Anika

By the same author
All in the Month of May

Anika

LINDA MARTIN

Apart from any fair dealing for the purposes of research or private study, or criticism or review, as permitted under the Copyright, Designs and Patents Act 1988, this publication may only be reproduced, stored or transmitted, in any form or by any means, with the prior permission in writing of the publishers, or in the case of reprographic reproduction in accordance with the terms of licences issued by the Copyright Licensing Agency. Enquiries concerning reproduction outside those terms should be sent to the publishers.

Matador
Unit 9 Priory Business Park
Kibworth Beauchamp
Leicester LE8 0RX, UK
Tel: (+44) 116 279 2299
Fax: (+44) 116 279 2277
Email: books@troubador.co.uk
Web: www.troubador.co.uk/matador

ISBN 978 1783064 601

British Library Cataloguing in Publication Data.
A catalogue record for this book is available from the British Library.

Typeset in 11pt Palatino by Troubador Publishing Ltd, Leicester, UK
Printed and bound in the UK by TJ International, Padstow, Cornwall

Matador is an imprint of Troubador Publishing Ltd

For Phyl and Roy

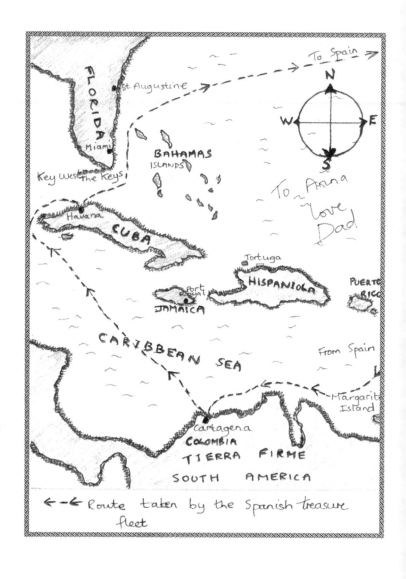

CHAPTER 1

The Caribbean, April 1668

Anika took a deep breath and plunged headfirst from the reef into the warm turquoise sea. The cannonball in her hands dragged her down, hair trailing like curly fronds of black seaweed, her shift dress clinging to cinnamon skin.

She kicked hard with bare legs and feet and her chest tightened as she swam down fifty feet towards the rainbow of plants and creatures that made the coral reef. As she descended her eardrums popped from the increase in pressure; she only had a few minutes underwater. A shoal of pink and yellow basslets flashed past in shimmering formation. She dropped the heavy ball as she spotted the pinctada oysters and tore them, one after another, from their sandy bed, thrusting each into the net bag tied to her belt. She pulled the cords tight, praying the shells contained pearls, and swam upwards to the circle of morning light.

Anika burst through the surface, gasping for air like a landed fish, and swept the hair from her eyes. They stung from the salty water. She shook her head to stop the ringing in her ears, then struck out for the rocks with a steady crawl stroke.

The sun burned the back of her head as she neared the coastline of Margarita Island, off Venezuela. The fishing boat, moored to an outcrop of rock off the shoreline, bobbed in the stiff breeze. She headed towards the red furled sail, her pace slowing as she drew nearer. An excellent swimmer, she had dived five times that morning, so now her limbs felt heavy and ached with the effort and her lungs were ready to burst. *I'm only twelve* she told herself. *I'll grow stronger.*

A shout from the boat and her stomach twisted. 'Why you so long?'

As Anika reached the boat a hairy arm hauled her out of the water and she sprawled on the decking alongside the writhing snapper and tuna. 'How many you got?' Antonio glared at her as she untied the bag from her belt, fighting for breath, and handed it to him. Her dark brown eyes, set wide and large, stared back. He untied the cords with his calloused hands, peered inside and cursed in Spanish. ' No many. I need set sail and look these after. You pray for pearls.'

I already have prayed, but she said nothing.

He threw the bag onto a heap of fishing nets, clambered off the boat onto the jutting rock and untied the rope. He was surprisingly agile for a big man with so much rum inside him. He jumped aboard, coiled the rope on the deck so that it looked like a sleeping cobra, hoisted the square sail, and took the tiller in the stern to steer a course. Anika hoped they would be home in Jamaica by dawn with this good westerly behind them.

She slumped back against the wooden hull as far away from him as she could get on the small boat, which was only yards. *When will I ever be free of this man?* He roped the tiller in place and fetched the oyster bag, then sat down on the decking with his back to the mast.

2

He pushed his straw hat back on his head and taking the dagger from his belt ran his finger down the blade and twisted it to watch the steel glint in the sunlight. A clash of pans came from the tiny cabin and he yelled, 'Diego hurry up with fish stew you lazy fool.'

He untied the oyster bag and spewed the shells onto the deck so that they rattled like shot. He hacked the first one open to find nothing but the salty creature within. He cursed, spat, then opened the next and the next and the next to more curses and as he opened the last whooped loudly. He took out a white tear-shaped pearl and held it up to the light, where it changed from pink to lilac to blue like a sparkling dewdrop at dawn.

His mood changed as swiftly as the weather in the Caribbean and he kicked out at the nets. 'This pearl good, but one in three month not make me rich man.' He spat towards the tuna on the deck, 'Fishing no make me rich man.' Anika half-listened as he repeated his usual complaint. 'The oysters fished so much hardly any pearls now and very rare you find the pink pearls in conch shells that make me rich man'

Anika said nothing. She rarely spoke aloud and when she did it was in English, as her father had taught her, though her mother spoke the West African Ashanti. She told Anika that when the mouth stumbles it is worse than the foot, so Anika watched people, listened and tried to understand. She was proud to be of mixed race. Antonio called her "mulatto", tawny skinned like a mule, but then he would.

She rose to her feet slowly, limbs like lead. The hot sun and warm wind had already dried her. She took the gourd hanging from the nail above the water barrel and drank until her thirst was quenched, dreaming of fresh coconut milk.

Antonio opened the leather purse he kept at his waist and dropped the pearl inside. He pulled the thongs tight and slumped back against the mast chewing at his fingernails, staring down at a discarded shell with the creature nestled inside. 'A pig no eat these pearl oysters,' then shouted at the cabin again, 'Diego dish the stew.'

Anika picked up a shell and turned it in the light, the nacre interior as lustrous and iridescent as the pearl it had contained, wondering how God created an oyster. She looked across at the stock of cannonballs she used in her dives and knew why men created those. She had seen much fighting in Port Royal.

A wiry little man stooped at the cabin door, his chest leathered from sailing. 'Fish stew, soon,' then wiped his brow with the back of his hand and ducked back into the cabin. Anika liked Diego, the Portuguese, because he was always kind to her. She heard the water pouring into the small cauldron hung over the galley fire and hoped he would add some allspice.

The salty smell of snapper and musky spice soon filled the boat and Anika's mouth watered. She thought about the pearl and how it would have grown more beautiful each day left in its own watery world. Antonio would sell it to a merchant as he had all the others, yet on a rich woman's skin the pearl 's lustre would fade, like her beauty.

Antonio shouted to Diego for the rum, which Diego brought out in a leather tankard. He drank greedily and wiped his mouth on his arm. Anika fetched spoons, and Diego emerged from a cloud of steam, like a genie from

4

a bottle, with two wooden bowls brimming with hot, watery stew. She ate hungrily soon finding it tasted vaguely of the snapper, but mostly of allspice.

When they had finished their meal Antonio's voice rang out again. 'Clear this deck and scrub girl. This boat it stinks.'

So do you, but she stood up to wet an old rag from the water barrel and soon rubbed hard at the decking, trying to lift the fish scales baked on the rosewood. The sun's heat grew more intense as she worked and she slowed. Her arm muscles ached even more and she thought longingly of her hammock in the house in Port Royal that she shared with her sick mother and Antonio. They had been at sea ten days now. She missed her Mama and hoped their neighbour Maria would look after her, so that the sleeping sickness would grow no worse.

She looked up from time to time to see Antonio lolling in the stern, steering the tiller. His eyes wore a glazed expression and were bloodshot, his face as veined and red as an onion. *Why had he come into their lives and ruined everything? He would have left with the other Spanish settlers when the English took Port Royal if he hadn't been in gaol at the time, for stealing a gold watch.*

She stared out to sea. *Was Diego frightened of him? Surely not.* She had seen Diego calm a maddened dog in Harbour Street, just by talking to him, and yet out here he skulked in the airless cabin like a hermit crab under a rock stirring his cauldron. Diego wore a mourning ring on his right hand, a skeleton inlaid, so must have lost somebody dear to him. Perhaps he thought about that person often.

She sprang to her feet and dropped the rag. Gripping

the rail until her knuckles turned white she watched the shark's fin as it made a bee line for the boat. Fear ripped her stomach as she remembered Daniel, her younger brother. He had gashed his arm on the keel of the boat when coming up from a dive. The shark had smelt his blood and dragged him down, turning the water red. She never saw him again and missed him every day.

Antonio would panic. She beckoned to Diego, put a finger to her lips and pointed to the sleek fin a few feet from the boat. He crossed the deck to the musket chest. The tiger shark lunged at the fish piled high on the deck, a gaping jaw showing rows of dagger teeth. Antonio backed away screaming. It lunged again, inches from his right leg.

As Diego aimed the musket Anika dashed forward, grabbed a large tuna and hurled it with all the force of her strong arms out to sea. The shark turned after it, and Diego lowered the musket. She slumped, exhausted, against the hull of the boat.

They sailed on north westerly, deep into the Caribbean Sea and as dusk fell swiftly she lay asleep.

* * *

Anika woke to Antonio's angry voice splitting the moonlight. 'Wake up girl. We're nearly there.'

She rubbed her eyes, yawned and immediately turned to the stern to check the lantern was out. Antonio had not lit it. Nobody would sail in Caribbean waters and draw attention to themselves, not even Antonio. This was pirate territory and there was safety in numbers, but they were alone.

She tensed at the thought and stayed alert, raking the silvery sea with tired eyes, listening for the sound of muffled oars in the wind. There was nothing out of the ordinary, just the wake of water behind them, the boat's creaking hull and the flap of the sail. She dozed and shortly woke again as the sea grew choppier.

Seeing a ship on the horizon Antonio fumbled for his precious spyglass. He passed it to her, 'You tell me. Your eyes better.'

She focused it quickly, confirming with few words that the ship was a Merchantman. Its topsails caught the blue light of the moon, but surely their fishing boat could not be seen. The ship sailed the same north westerly course as them and ploughed on. Antonio let out a sigh and they sailed into the night to the south east coast of Jamaica.

The lights of Port Royal twinkled like diamonds and beckoned Anika home. They reached the natural harbour at dawn and found it crammed with ships, large and small. They sailed through the narrow entrance and passed Fort Charles, the stone fortress named after the English King Charles II, the port itself also named for him. The strains of drunken singing, shouts, dogs barking, breaking glass reached her ears and for the first time in days Anika smiled. She had lived in this rich and rowdy city all her life and loved the place. The Blue Mountains stood firm in the distance, their foothills skirting the port.

As Antonio tied up the boat at the wharf four Englishmen jumped aboard calling to Antonio. Anika recognised them as his drinking companions. They wore long black wigs and velvet frockcoats, gold chains about their necks. Pistols gleamed from the silk sashes hung from their shoulders and she knew them to be pirates.

He embraced them like long-lost friends and quickly offered rum. Anika knew he must do this since Spaniards were hated by the English. They accepted the tankards, then without warning the stocky one with a scar on the back of his right hand put a pistol to Antonio's temple, and nodded towards Anika. 'We need the girlie tomorrow evenin', Cap'n's orders 'cos we sail on the tide.'

Anika knew Antonio would sell his mother into slavery and she froze with fear. 'Of course you take the girl Signor Gibbons. Do what you want with her.' Sensing profit he pleaded in a strangled voice, 'Can I come?'

'You might be useful. Some of the charts are in Spanish. Bring her with you to the "Black Lady" tomorrow,' and he waved the pistol towards the largest ship moored further along the harbour. It flew the "Jolly Roger" flag, the skull-and-crossbones. Gibbons then pointed the pistol towards Diego as he came out from the cabin reeking of allspice. 'Can he cook English food?'

Antonio nodded. 'Yes. He very good. '

'Bring him too.'

Anika would have loved to run rather than go with these men but she knew that she would not. A short distance away Mama lay ill in her hammock and she would never leave her. So she and Antonio headed for home, a small two storeyed house in New Street in the centre of the pirate city.

Antonio untied his leather purse and looking around him like a thief, he groped for the pearl and held it up to the rays of the new day.

CHAPTER 2

The Caribbean Sea, April 1668

Anika grabbed a leather bucket and climbed the creaking ladder to the main deck of the English Merchantman, "Black Lady". She climbed the next ladder and up through the open hatch onto the weather deck. Crossing to the starboard she put down the bucket and rested her bare arms on the rail, staring out at the rippled blue Caribbean Sea and the cloudless sky.

She took a deep breath of morning air and tasted salt on her lips; bliss after the scorching heat and wood smoke of the galley. Nearly a week at sea had passed since her return to Port Royal and she worked with Diego in the cramped galley kitchen.

The wind ruffled her hair and cooled her skin, as her white shift blew around her knees and her bare feet hugged the warm deck. The ship scythed through the sea and she steadied herself against its roll. She had come to love " Black Lady", but not those who sailed her. On her first day one of the pirates had boasted that the ship had been captured a year before and Captain Jameson had re-named her "Black Lady" after his lover. The ship's bell had been cast in gold only this year and engraved with the name.

Shielding her eyes from the fierce sun she stared up at the "Jolly Roger" flag streaming out from the top of the mainmast. If half the stories these men told were true they were to be feared. They moaned that it was bad luck to have a female aboard and they kept their distance from her. At least she slept on the orlop deck, near the galley, away from their snoring and farting in the fo'c's'le.

Some ordinary seamen had been captured from merchant and Navy vessels and forced onto the ship, offered piracy or a slow death. She certainly had no choice but to come aboard and tried hard not to think of her Mama, who was no worse, yet no better.

The square sails filled by the north-easterly trade winds billowed above like giants' hammocks hung out to dry. Pirates climbed the ratlines of the shrouds towards the main yard to trim the canvas, wearing only dirty calico trousers and red turbans, knives stuffed in their rope belts.

Reluctantly she picked up the bucket, carried it over to the water barrels by the mainmast and lowered it into the nearest barrel. She raised the bucket of water and stood it on the deck. Jack Simpson cheered from the crow's nest as he replaced "The Jolly Roger" with the flag of Saint George, ensuring they were not recognised as a pirate vessel, but as an English Merchantman. The pirate crew bragged that they were buccaneers and with their noses up, like hounds after the fox, chased the Spanish treasure fleet, searching for riches beyond their dreams.

Antonio said the Spanish treasure fleet hoped to beat the hurricane season, which raged from June to November. It had not long sailed from Havana in Cuba back home to Cadiz in Spain, with galleons loaded to the gunwales with gold , silver and precious jewels. "Black Lady" had sailed many leagues, so that they were now in reach of East Florida and the treasure fleet.

The voices of the pirates in the rigging drifted down to her. 'Watch yersel' Jimmy. You're no up a wee ladder buildin' a hoose.'

His brother shouted down. 'Mind yersel Robbie 'cos I can climb as well as the next mun.'

Sam, the gunner, called over to the pair of them. 'Thank yer lucky stars yer not in the Navy. They'd 'ave us up 'ere in all weathers and a whippin for not doin' it quick enough when yer get down'

Sean Murphy, thin and gangly as an Irish scarecrow, piped up. 'So long as I get me whole share of the treasure. I got two turds on me last ship.'

The men roared with laughter. He hung from the rigging, a spider's web of hemp rope, wondering what they were laughing about, then they began to sing a shanty about the girls in the ports.

Anika noticed the cabin boy mending a sail on the quarterdeck above. He looked down, flushed, then up again, a pleasant smile on his tanned face, curly blonde hair tousled by the wind. He was English and older than her, possibly fourteen or fifteen. The folds of canvas spread about him like a never-ending story, patched and torn, patched.

The shanty petered out and she heard Sam's voice again as he stared down at the cabin boy. 'Nobody was allowed on the quarterdeck 'cept the Cap'n in the Navy. When I was…'

Jimmy shouted back at him. 'Och nay more on the Navy, mun. You're no in the Navy now.'

Sam said no more and the singing started up again.

Captain Jameson came out on deck, followed by Gibbons. Anika remembered how Gibbons had held a pistol to Antonio's head and shivered in spite of the heat. They stood nearby and had not seen her behind the water barrel. There were portraits of King Charles II everywhere in Port Royal and wearing his black curly wig Captain Jameson looked like him, every inch the commander, tall and lean, in a knee-length scarlet frockcoat and breeches, all embroidered with gold thread. Silver buckles shone on his pointed black shoes.

He turned to his 'First Officer', so-called after the Royal Navy rankings and spoke in the honeyed voice of an English gentleman. 'We shall soon be near the wreck as the reefs are close by.' He played with the lace at his cuffs as he spoke. 'Spanish treasure Gibbons, gold and silver, jewels that will make your eyes pop.'

'You're a sea artist Cap'n and can map us a course blindfolded.' Gibbons' grey eyes did not match the affection in his voice and he looked about him, like a cornered wolf. His chin sprouted grey stubble and he wore a heavy gold necklace around his neck. The green velvet coat pulled against his body.

The Captain smiled at the compliment. ' I was trained as a navigator Gibbons by England's finest, the great Royal Navy, but ran into a bit of trouble with the Navy Board you know and decided to part company in Guinea.' His blue eyes twinkled with fun. 'As for the wrecked Spanish galleon, the girl can dive and find it. It's only as deep as those pearls she dives for. If we train a musket on her she'll dive.'

They both laughed.

Anika closed her eyes and took a deep breath. So that was it; they had not brought her on board just to help in the galley. Her stomach tightened and she thought she would be sick.

Jameson pressed his index finger to his lips. 'Snug's the word until I tell the men.' He smiled.' We attacked the galleon three weeks ago while you were away with that rogue Henry Morgan helping the English fight the Dutch.'

Gibbons nodded, 'That I was Cap'n.'

Then Jameson's eyes grew cold and his voice quieter. He looked hard at Gibbons. 'I leave it to Henry Morgan to fight English wars, not my men.'

Gibbons looked down, 'Yes Cap'n.'

Jameson stared out towards the horizon. 'The galleon, "Don Carlos", sailed alone, an excellent prize, probably separated from the treasure fleet in a storm some time after it left Havana. We took it easily; the crew surrendered at the sight of us.' He threw back his head and laughed. 'It carried hordes of Peruvian gold and silver loaded in Cartagena and was on its way home to Spain.'

'Half our crew prepared to sail it on into the Gulf Stream and back around to Port Royal. We were to follow, but we hadn't loaded the treasure before we were caught in a storm.'

Anika listened, keeping perfectly still.

'We escaped but watched the Spanish galleon go down, run aground on the reef over there.' He pointed out to the port side.

'What if we can't find the wreck Cap'n?'

'We'll sail straight on for our island of Tortuga. Best

not wait around these waters for storms. We'll careen the old girl and meet up with friends, then we'll try our luck from there; pursue the account and take the treasure.'

Gibbons nodded and Jameson turned to go. 'Charts to study. Keep an eye on the crew,' and he crossed to the hatch and climbed down into the belly of the ship. Gibbons turned, sullen-faced, to watch the men up in the rigging. A few of them spotted him and the singing they had begun once more died away. He spat on to the deck.

Anika picked up the bucket of water, spilling some, and climbed the steps to the quarterdeck to talk to the cabin boy. Perhaps she would tell him what was to happen to her. Gibbons inspected the swivel gun mounted on the ship's rail and patting it like a pet hound shouted up to Sam, 'Give this murderer a clean and look sharp about it.'

As he turned away Sam shook his fist at him. The cabin boy stirred an imaginary ladle with his right hand and she nodded and smiled. Gibbons moved away to the sand glass, checking the watch time.

Anika sat down next to the boy, who continued his sewing, a little red in the face. She noticed he wore a leather palm to protect his right hand as he forced the needle through the sail. His hands were not roughened like those of the other seamen. He spoke quietly, 'I live in Port Royal too. Sean told me they'd picked you up there. I work in Jameson's tavern as a pot-boy.'

She understood he was probably little more than a slave and found herself saying, 'I miss Mama. She's not well,' wondering why she had told her deepest secret to

14

this boy she hardly knew. She would not tell him the Captain was to force her to dive on the wreck.

'I'm sorry for your Mama.' He looked up as the men clambered down the rigging. 'When the Cap'n goes on his raids he brings me along as cabin boy. I suppose they wanted you for the galley work.'

Gibbons heard him talking and he shouted up, 'Get on with yer work unless yer want a whippin'.' The sails cracked in the gathering breeze and he span around, hand on his dagger.

Anika stared down at him and thought of a fat-bellied toad. There was a story that he had hacked off a woman's fingers to get at her rings. Sam said that he was a sailor who had been charged with attempting to strangle his wife in a tavern in London and had been transported to work on one of the sugar plantations in Barbados. Pirates raided it for African slaves to sell and he was also taken, very soon joining their crew.

Gibbons rang the ship's bell at the end of half an hour on the sand glass then turned it and went below where they heard him slapping Antonio. 'All you had to do was fish and turn the hour glass, you lazy….'

Anika turned back towards the boy.

He looked at her intently. 'My name's Stephen, Stephen Cartwright.

'Anika Green, I fish every day with Antonio and sometimes we sail to Margarita Island for the pearl fishing. We scrape a living.' Gibbons came back on deck and Anika knew she must return to the galley.

She went further into the ship, desperately trying not to spill the water in the bucket, the stench from the filthy water in the bilge grew stronger and made her

15

feel sick again and she spotted another rat slinking into the shadows. They were black, large as small cats and their red eyes seemed to follow her everywhere.

As she entered the galley Diego's fish stew simmered in the huge copper cauldron hanging over the brick furnace. She put down the bucket thankfully and rubbed her sore arm.

The heat seemed more intense after her spell on deck; the smoke got into her throat and made her cough and the steam made it difficult to see. Diego handed her a knife and pointed at a pile of yams waiting to be peeled, then poured more water into his stew.

She wiped the sweat from her forehead and dropped sliced yams into the pot, stirring them with the wooden ladle. She added a little too much pepper and sneezed, disturbing another rat, who scuttled over the fish guts in the corner.

Suddenly cries went up, one after another, like waves crashing on the seashore, all the way to the galley.

'Gibbons is stabbed.'

'Fetch the surgeon.'

'Gibbons is murdered.'

Anika and Diego rushed up through the ship to the weather deck. Gibbons lay sprawled on his back, eyes wide open, blood spreading over his shirt. A semi-circle of men stood silently around him.

Jameson looked down at the man's staring eyes and wiped the dagger of blood with his lace handkerchief. He handed the blood-stained cloth to Sam, 'Toss him overboard and make sure you weigh him down. He got above himself so I had to kill him.' He looked around at the crew and they laughed nervously. Anika saw the fear in their eyes. They all hated Gibbons but only Jameson could have done this.

He walked away with Gerald, the fat-bellied surgeon. 'Not much profit for you there Gerald,' and he laughed.

Gerald laughed too and closed his canvas case of gruesome knives and syringes and thrust it into his coat pocket.

Jameson turned back and stopped. 'Jimmy McDougal. Will you be my First Officer?'

Jimmy sprang forward. 'Och aye Cap'n. I canny think of anything better.' He looked like a man who had discovered a treasure chest when he had been digging a grave.

Jameson smiled and went up on the quarterdeck with Gerald waddling behind like an overfed spaniel.

As the sun lowered, Anika ate her stew with Stephen out on the weather deck. The sky was a bruise of purples, reds and mauves and a stiff breeze blew from the east. They talked of Gibbons' murder.

Stephen swallowed another watery mouthful and winced at the peppery taste. 'Everyone hated him, but for Jameson to kill him like that in cold-blood. I've seen him in sword fights in the tavern, but never just kill a man.' Stephen shook his head. 'I keep a journal and that is by far the most interesting entry. Whatever made him do it?'

Anika spoke slowly, not used to airing her thoughts. 'I think he did it to show he's in control of the ship, so that the men will fear him.'

Stephen looked at her for a moment and nodded.

They sat and talked of life in Port Royal. She found herself telling him about Antonio and her mother. 'There's nothing I can do. He helped her when she first arrived in Port Royal and has wormed his way into her life.'

A cry of delight came from Captain Jameson as he stood at the port rail and focused his spyglass. He took it from his eye and called to Jimmy. 'Bring the men together. Fetch up the watch below from the fo'c's'le and tell Sean Murphy to bring his fiddle.'

'Right 'way Cap'n.'

He returned to the spyglass. It was a beautiful instrument inlaid with gold, catching the fading sunlight. He shouted after Jimmy, 'And bring the waggoner. I want to check the chart again. We're getting dangerously close to the reef .'

'Aye aye Cap'n.' Jimmy McDougal hurried off, chewing on his tobacco.

Soon the weather deck swarmed with the men, all dressed to impress, their pistols and cutlasses gleaming. There were forty at least, laughing, swigging rum, arguing; Gibbons already forgotten. Many were bearded or unshaven, dressed in velvet coats and lace shirts, often too big for them, or too small. Some had the star-shaped scars of smallpox on their faces other with limbs or eyes lost to the chase. They wore bright sashes around their waists, reds, blues, golds and across their shoulders hung leather baldrics or ribbons to proudly sling their weapons.

To Anika they seemed like squawking parrots, happiest when up on the rigging, perched high above the water they disliked, arguing over pecking order, jawing and yawing. Few of them could swim as it was thought unlucky in a seaman. They were like the gentlemen merchants in Port Royal, yet they gambled with their lives as well as the roll of a dice.

They quietened as the Captain raised his spyglass to his eye. 'A small ship gentlemen, on the horizon. It's certainly Spanish by her colours and may well be a salvage ship looking for the wreck of the Spanish galleon, the "Don Carlos". You all remember her I'm sure. Well, shall we take the little Spanish ship, unburden her of her cargo and then search for the wreck? Raise your tankards if you agree.'

The men let out loud cheers and raised their tankards.

'Take out your clay pipes gentlemen and we will smoke God's own tobacco. You have done well not to smoke below and cause us a fire. You Joseph,' he turned to the tall, angular quartermaster, 'must ensure everything is taken from the salvage ship and loaded in our hold.'

'Yes Cap'n.' He bowed low and took out a leather-bound notebook, pen and ink and began scribbling.

Jameson turned towards Anika and said coldly, 'And you girl will dive and find the wreck.' She nodded and looked at Stephen, reading the dismay in his eyes.

Jameson beckoned Diego, who handed him a glass of red wine. 'Modyford, the Governor of Port Royal, to those who don't know the wretched man, wants us to join him in his English wars against the Dutch; take settlements and plantations on their Caribbean islands. That is no life for a pirate, unless your name is Gibbons.' He stared hard at them and they tried, and in some cases failed, to meet his eyes. 'We are not hired soldiers to die at the hands of the Dutch. We make our own chances and live by our own rules. We light no lanterns tonight.'

There were more cheers and raised tankards.

'For the benefit of the new crew a reminder of the rules on the loot. We share the spoils of course, but as Captain I get two and a half share.' He nodded to the new carpenter, 'but three quarters share only for you Jed because you're not risking your life.'

Jed sprawled drunk by the railing grinning like a madman, his red and green parrot hopping up and down the ship's rail squawking, 'Yes Cap'n Yes Cap'n.' He never left Jed, often perching on his shoulder. Anika hoped the ship would not need major repairs as she watched Jed struggle to his feet and strike off the top of an earthenware beer bottle with his cutlass, nearly killing himself. The parrot hopped closer to him.

The Captain shook his head and turned towards Anika and Stephen. 'You two get half shares and if we're caught you'll be set free as youngsters.'

They nodded.

'The rest of us will dance the hempen jig at low-tide.' He put his hand to his throat and dropped his head like a man hanging, then suddenly threw his head up and grinned. 'Unless we pay off a few worthy judges.' He smiled around at the crew who chuckled and sniggered. 'Unlike the foolish landsmen, who've never put to sea, us seadogs know a thing or two about the world.'

'You Gerald get one and half share as the ship's surgeon, except we all pray we won't be needing you because you'll probably kill us anyway!'

Sniggers again as Gerald nodded at the Captain, his belly moving at the same time under his blood-stained frockcoat.

'Jameson paced up and down the deck. 'If you lose an arm, a leg, an eye each has its price. It's all written down in the articles we signed, but sometimes we all need reminding. You'd get six hundred pieces of eight or six slaves for a lost right arm.' He looked around him happily, 'I look after my men.'

Another murmur of approval.

'So we are agreed. We take the Spanish ship, salvage the wreck and then sail back to Tortuga and our brethren of the coast. We'll kill a few turtles and pigs, have a feast and bury some of the treasure for our old age. Then after a rest we shall fly at high game.'

Gerald looked baffled.

' A falconry term Gerald. We will take more treasure ships, prizes, and finally sail for Port Royal.'

There was a roar from the men. Anika shook her head and exchanged looks with Stephen.

Jed, the carpenter, stirred himself and slurred, 'To the Cap'n.'

The men shouted, 'To the Cap'n.'

Jed's parrot squawked, 'To the Cap'n' and the pirates roared with laughter.

CHAPTER 3

In the early hours of the morning, under a watery moon, "Black Lady" changed course and sailed towards the Spanish salvage ship. Anika and Stephen knelt on the main deck next to the cannon, tense and fidgety, ready to roll up kegs of gunpowder and pass cannonballs to Sam and the other gunners. The men had stowed their hammocks and pushed sea chests to the hull walls, leaving the deck eerily empty.

Sam tore off his blue jacket and rolled up his sleeves. 'We're only lightly armed. We've the six cannon here, Sean Murphy at the sternchaser and four swivel guns aloft, but by keeping the weight down we've got the advantage of speed.' His face betrayed his optimism. Deep worry lines scored his forehead, as though years in the Navy had taught him one thing only; that he could do nothing right. 'A team of Navy gunners can load and fire every few minutes so we'd be dead meat against a Navy warship.

'The order is to fire only if fired upon. The lads should be able to take the ship by stealth, boarding her unseen and not need the cannon.' He took a gold necklace from his leather satchel, kissed it and hung it around his neck.

Anika was primed and ready, like the cannon, and heard everything from the sea swell and creaking of the ship's oak timbers to the muffled voices of the men. She jumped as she heard ropes grating on the side of the hull, then a splash and another splash. Stephen smiled at her encouragingly and she smiled back.

Sam 's voice croaked with excitement. 'Our lads are lowering the pinnaces. If they're spotted we're all dead men. The Spaniards have twenty cannon at least judging by their gun ports.'

Anika peered through the unlatched gun port and beckoned to Stephen. Each of the two small boats carried a dozen crew members, Jameson in the bow of one and Jimmy McDougal in the other. As they rowed across to the Spanish ship in a choppy sea, there was barely a sound as they pulled on their oars and drew closer to the prey.

They hooked grappling irons to her stern. Anika turned at the creak of wheels to see Sean train the heavy carriage gun in the stern on the Spanish ship, ready to fire if the men were spotted.

The pirates shinned up the ropes. Some used axes to help them climb the high wooden wall, carved and painted intricately to display Spanish wealth. One man was left in each pinnace. All the others were aboard her in minutes streaming over the deck, weapons at the ready.

A musket shot split the air and a figure fell to the deck. There were cries and shouts, followed by more shots. Fierce fighting broke out on the deck, hand to hand with whirling cutlasses, metal ringing on metal. Anika heard screams, an explosion, and saw a flash of white.

As the pirates chopped through the sail lifts with their axes, the mainsail fell to the deck. They jammed the rudder so that the ship could not get away. It was all over within half an hour, a turn of the sand glass, and they had not fired one cannon. Anika and Stephen hurried up on deck to await their return.

Jimmy shortly clambered out of the first pinnace and up the rope ladder to report that they had indeed taken a Spanish salvage ship. 'She sailed from Saint Augustine in East Florida two days ago, to haul up the treasure from the sunken "Don Carlos". We've killed a deal of 'em and we've left the rest away doon in their hold with three of ours guardin' 'em. They're caged up like monkeys and their Spanish Cap'n is spittin' blood, trussed up like a wee hen.'

As dawn broke, the buccaneers returned to "Black Lady" jubilant, leaving the same men behind to guard the Spanish prisoners. They spent much of the morning on the weather deck getting drunk on a heady mixture of rum and Spanish wine. Anika watched Sean sprinkle gunpowder in his tankard to make a "kill-devil".

They sang and jigged around the weather deck to the sound of Sean's fiddle and Jimmy's drum. Sean danced like a scarecrow come to life, thin arms holding the fiddle on his shoulder, fingers all over the strings, legs jerking in opposite directions. Raising his black leather tankard the surgeon called out to him, 'You're not much of a sailor Murphy but you surely can fiddle. Every ship should have a musician aboard.' They finally sprawled around the deck senseless, all thoughts of retrieving any treasure from the sunken galleon gone.

As Anika made her way down to the galley to prepare salted beef for those who could stand, she thought of nothing else. *Could she dive that deep?*

As the day wore on the quartermaster, Joseph, ordered her into his pinnace with Stephen and six of the crew to fetch food and wine from the prize ship. Supplies loaded,

Anika rowed hard on the return trip, arm muscles strong through hours of swimming. The pinnace sat low in the water, weighed down with jars of olive oil, wine casks, sacks of yams and sweet-smelling oranges.

Ahead of them was the other pinnace loaded with sails and ropes, more sacks of vegetables and a coop of hens clucking and trying to fly. She heard Joseph yelling orders to load the goods to the port side of 'Black Lady.' She knew it to be a seaman's superstition that cargo should tilt the ship to the port for a successful voyage, but was not sure that she believed it. Jimmy sat in the stern holding a dagger to the Spanish Captain' s throat.

Both pinnaces came alongside and Captain Jameson called down cheerily to the beaten Captain as he climbed the ladder, 'Welcome aboard, Sir.' He swept off his feathered hat and made a mock bow. Anika and the rest of the crew followed up the ladder and back on deck stared at the defiant Spanish Captain.

He stood proudly on the deck and adjusted his yellow silk coat, then glared at Jameson. He spoke in fast Spanish and gestured wildly.

Jameson turned to Jimmy and laughed out loud. 'A bumble bee in a cow pat thinks himself a king.'

The men laughed and Jimmy handed Jameson a pair of white leather gauntlets. 'Thought you might like these Cap'n. If he canny find the wreck he won't have nay hands fer his fine gloves.'

Anika knew he meant it.

Jameson thumped Jimmy on the back and laughed. He took the gauntlets and pulled them on, admiring the soft calfskin. This brought another outpouring of Spanish from the distressed Spanish Captain.

Jameson laughed again and turned to Jimmy. 'Fetch Antonio to translate. I need to know the exact location of the shipwreck.'

Antonio hurried up to Jameson and bowed slightly. 'Yes Signor, how can I help?'

Anika could hardly bear to look at him.

'Translate every word I say.' Jameson pulled a pistol from his belt and held it to the Spanish Captain's head. His voice grew measured, icy. 'If you want to see another dawn, you'll take me out to the spot where the ship went down. If we find no wreck you die.'

Antonio translated.

The Spaniard spoke even faster and Jameson threw back his head and laughed again. 'His tongue runs on wheels. What does he say?'

Antonio's cheeks puffed out. 'He say that he is Captain Felipe Ramirez and he sent to salvage the ship "Don Carlos". The treasure galleon went straight down to ocean floor without breaking up and one of the masts was seen just above the water, but another storm drove first salvage ship away and when they come back mast he is gone.'

Jameson ran his finger along the silver scroll work on the pistol. 'Throw him in the boat.' He looked around the weather deck and beckoned to Anika. 'You girl, get ready to dive and I need four rowers and the two Spanish divers from the salvage ship.'

Antonio took Anika roughly by the arm and dragged her to the rope ladder, showing his ownership.

Jameson put the pistol to her temple and whispered in her ear. 'You find that wreck or you're shark's meat.'

He turned to Jimmy. 'We leave now.'

Anika picked up a cannonball, prayed for her Mama and dived from the pinnace. The two boy divers hired by the Spanish followed her. The water was crystal clear and she kicked and swam down towards the sand bank. Anemones anchored to the coral formed swathes of vivid pinks and deep blues and waved in the current. Shoals of black and yellow angelfish darted past her.

Sea anemones, like quill pens, feathered her hands as she searched and they glowed at her touch, as though she were invited to pluck one and write. There was no sign of the shipwreck and her lungs began to scream for air. She dropped the ball and swam for the surface.

All afternoon she dived around the reef and found nothing. The Spanish divers also found nothing. Each time she surfaced her anxiety grew, until silently they rowed back to "Black Lady." She feared Jameson more than she had ever feared anyone. Back on the ship the drinking and singing had stopped.

Jameson swept down to his great cabin in the stern and shouted to Anika as he passed, 'Fetch me rum and something to eat.'

Anika scrambled down the ladder and hurried to the galley, where she found Diego stirring the cauldron. *Not fish?* He had killed four of the chickens and stirred the jointed birds in the pot and now poured in most of the red wine, draining the bottle himself.

He winked at her and handed over a hunk of cheese. She smiled at him but shook her head. The shelves lay heaped with carrots, potatoes, hens' eggs, all taken from the freshly provisioned Spanish ship. He poured them each a small beer and handed one to her. 'You will find it and then we shall go home to Jamaica. Have a cackle-fruit.' He handed her a hard- boiled egg and counted out the rest. She might eat it later.

Chicken and eggs, what a feast for the crew; no hard tack biscuits today. She pocketed the egg and made her way to the great cabin with the Captain's silver plate, inscribed with the initials RJ, piled with boiled chicken, egg, potatoes and peas, a goblet of wine in her other hand. Putting down the wine, she knocked and heard him call her in.

She entered a glittering palace, ten times larger than the galley. His sea-chest stood in the corner, open and glinting with gold and silver coins, and jewels, daring anyone to touch them. His pistols lay on the table next to his charts, astrolabe and ivory bound compass. Brocade coats and breeches lay strewn over chairs. What a peacock!

A portrait hung on the wall paneling to the side of him. It was a large oil painting in a gilt frame of a beautiful white-skinned woman, long black curls framing her oval face. She wore a low-cut black satin gown with a necklace of pearls to match the teardrop ear-rings. Her brown eyes looked sad and thoughtful. *She must be the Black Lady.*

His voice broke into her thoughts as she placed the plate of food next to his knife and spoon. He, too, looked at the painting. 'When a woman wears diamonds it is they that sparkle, but when she wears pearls it is she who shines.' Anika stared at him, challenging. She believed it was a pure soul that shone, not pearls, and thought of her Mama.

He stared back at her as she placed the goblet of red

wine on the table and spoke carelessly, 'Gibbons was no great loss. He was cruel to the men.'

She bowed her head ready to leave, reading his mind.

'Look at me girl.'

She did as he asked, questioning him with thoughtful eyes.

He took a long drink from his goblet and placed it back on the table, admiring the sparkling rubies set in its base. 'At your age I was a waterman on the River Thames with my father, a foul- mouthed monster I loathed. I can still smell the black mud of that river at ebb tide as we rowed passengers across,' and he wrinkled his nose. 'Then I joined the Navy at thirteen and now I am a great Captain,' and he played with the heavy gold chains hung around his neck. 'You dive before sunset and fetch me more wine.'

She nodded, but would not look at him again as she left the cabin.

* * *

As ordered, while the light was good, Anika and the Spanish boys prepared to dive. She was sure Jameson was looking in the wrong place, but she did as she was told. She had little choice. *Could it be that the Spanish Captain was misleading them? He was risking his life and that of all his remaining crew if he was, or could he be mistaken in the location? The Spaniards clearly thought their lost treasure ship was there somewhere.*

They rowed to the furthest side of the reef and Anika dived again. This time she held her breath even longer and swam along the side of the reef, dropping the cannonball into the swaying sea grasses. She swam down and the water grew colder, doubting the boys could follow her at this depth. A green turtle skimmed past her, seeming to fly under the water, its broad front flippers like wings.

A school of spotted dolphins swam around her, somersaulting, playing. She studied the white sand and saw a crab's feathery antennae and the tail of a burrowing fish. Something else lay in the white sand and thrusting in her hand her long fingers clasped metal.

She pulled a gold necklace from its soft grave. The dolphins swam away and as she watched them swim deeper she saw it. Thirty yards away at least, ghostly, the broken hull of the galleon lay on its side on a sand bank, pretending to be a coral reef. Shoals of fish swirled about and claimed it as their home.

Her lungs fought for air as she strove for the surface, the necklace clamped in her hand. As she neared the keel of the pinnace one of the boys swam towards her and tried to grab the necklace. She fought and kicked but he snatched it from her hand.

She burst through the surface to see the Spanish boy hold up the necklace in triumph. She spluttered out water, her throat and nostrils burning with the salt and no words came, but her eyes shone as she looked across at Stephen. *Could he guess that she had found "Don Carlos"?*

He put his shirt around her and she saw that he was anxious that she could hardly get her breath. The crew were wild with joy, thumping the Spaniard on the back, offering him their rum, all talking at once.

Jameson smiled and took the necklace, admiring the thick gold links. 'Gold and jewels last for all time not like pretty pearls, which fade and crumble. This will go in the ship's treasure chest.' He looked around him. 'You all know the rules. Anyone caught stealing from there has their nose and ears slit.' He pulled a dagger in front of his nose. 'Tomorrow you three dive again and we will find the galleon.'

Then as she got her breath back a smile spread across her face. *The Spanish boys could dive no deeper than thirty feet and would never find it. It was her galleon. However much Jameson made her dive she would not find it. He would have to kill her first and she knew that she was more useful to him alive. They would never know how deep she dived, even Antonio did not know.*

She looked up at the black clouds gathering to the west and remembered what her mother had told her about making plans for the future. The pinnace now rocked dangerously in the choppy water as the wind strengthened. The first drops of rain splashed her hands as the sky lowered. Jameson sniffed the air and frowned at the leaden sky. 'Pull for the "Black Lady". Once this weather passes we shall find the "Don Carlos".'

The pinnace drew alongside the pirate ship and they all struggled up the swinging rope ladder, as the rain lashed down. 'Jameson bellowed to the crew to reef the sails and the men scrambled up the rigging and fought with the heavy wet canvas. Anika and the rowers hauled up the pinnace with the pulleys and block and tackle as the ship lurched and the rope burned her palms.

* * *

As the evening drew on the tropical storm arrived like a raging demon. The wind howled around them and a lightning flash was quickly followed by the roll of thunder, another flash and a boom of thunder directly overheard. They could do nothing but sit it out. Florida was close, but so were the reefs.

Anika struggled up to the weather deck and secured the chicken coop with ropes as best she could. She held fast to the rigging as the waves topped the rails. About a hundred yards off the Spanish salvage ship tossed wildly in the churning sea. 'All below except the watch,' screamed Jameson above the screeching wind. 'Batten down the hatches and pump out this water. Throw the guns over and lighten her, so we rise.' Anika wove her way down the ladder to the main deck, salt stinging her mouth. She grabbed onto a metal hook on the hull wall as the ship pitched violently.

The sea roared and smashed against the wooden hull and as she lurched across the deck she was thrown heavily against the barrels of gunpowder, which dislodged and crashed around. She staggered over to her hammock in the fo'c's'le and pulled a thick cloth from her canvas bag and dried herself, before setting off for the galley to fasten down what she could.

A mammoth wave hit the ship on the starboard and they were yawing, turning over, going down. The deck filled with water up to her knees, then over her waist and she swam towards the gun port and wrenched it open. She took a deep breath and ducked through and out of the sinking ship into swirling waters. Barrels and pulleys and shattered timbers threatened to beat her into an early grave, but she ducked and dodged and swam and swam upwards, minutes passing.

Finally she made it up into a wild sea. There was the

salvage ship tossing in the swell and she swam for it with every last ounce of her strength, hauled herself up the ladder, and collapsed on the deck unconscious.

* * *

Anika woke next day and looked up at a blue shield of sky. Stephen smiled down at her where she lay on the deck with his frockcoat for a pillow. 'We are sailing for Port Royal in the Spanish salvage ship. The Spaniards are prisoners below. Diego, myself and six of the crew who survived are sailing her. When you feel up to it we could do with some of your fish stew.'

'But what…'

"Black Lady" went down in the storm and we are the only survivors. You will never see Jameson again; so few of them could swim. Now there are two wrecks down there.'

Anika slowly sat up, her body a rack of pain. 'We'll go back one day soon Stephen and find the wrecks and I shall dive on them. It is my dream and we should all chase our dreams.' Now if I can find some food left on here I will make us a wonderful stew.' She stood up, smiling.

Her smile faded as she spotted Antonio slumped against the rail on the quarterdeck, chewing his fingernails.

CHAPTER 4

April 2013, London

The historical detective, Dr James Robertson, sat at a desk in the British Library, leather-bound books and old maps strewn around the computer screen. He ran his hands through his tight black hair and yawned. He peered over the top of his glasses and smiled at his daughter Anna, who had just joined him for lunch after her Saturday morning shopping trip with her Aunt Julie. 'A whole week's work and I've found nothing.'

Anna squeezed his arm. 'Never mind Dad better luck next week.' Anna thought that the tight-lipped woman to his right could have turned them both to stone as she glared at them. *Surely multicultural England could deal with Jamaican looks.*

He was mad on finding this old Spanish galleon, the "Don Carlos." She loved it when he got all enthusiastic about his work, like a boy solving an adventure mystery, an Indiana Jones. He took off his reading glasses and rubbed his eyes. As he scraped back the chair the woman let out a deep sigh. Ignoring her, he looked at the carrier bags and grinned.

She shrugged her shoulders. 'I'd got nothing to wear.'

They returned the books and maps then wandered down the stairs to the restaurant, where he ordered freshly made tuna baguettes, a pot of tea for one and a banana smoothie. 'Want a bun? '

Anna smiled up at him, her features like his; the wide mouth and deep brown eyes, the broad nose. She was twelve and he was a slightly-worn forty.

Settled at the table eating lunch, he talked of his recent visit to Seville in Spain. Anna listened, munching through the Chelsea bun; sugary icing deliciously sweet in her mouth, saving the glace' cherry until last. 'After days of trawling through seventeenth century documents in old Castilian script in the archive centre I only found one reference to the "Don Carlos". It sank off East Florida in April, 1668 and a salvage ship was sent to the wreck site by order of the Spanish king, Carlos II. There was no sign of the ship's inventory, which lists the cargo of treasure.

'I do have a letter, dated 16 May 1668, written by a survivor, a Spanish priest. It's to his mother.' He pulled a crumpled photocopy from his jacket pocket and put on his glasses.

'He describes how the galleon became separated from the treasure fleet in a storm after they sailed from Havana in Cuba, March 1668. It was attacked and taken by a pirate ship, " Black Lady." Half the pirate crew prepared to sail the galleon and its treasure back to Port Royal in Jamaica when a storm blew up and wrecked the "Don Carlos" on the reef.'

He scanned the letter written in a spidery black ink. 'The priest doesn't say what happened to the pirate ship but he swam to the pinnace and along with a handful of others landed on a tiny island, which could be Key West, Florida. He describes the ship's location when the storm hit and it sounds like the Lower Keys, but I've no idea how accurate that is.'

Anna stared at the black writing. *How could he understand it?*

He sipped his tea and frowned. 'It's odd because the Spanish kept excellent records in Seville and I can't believe they didn't keep an inventory.' He shook his head, then looked up smiling. 'We could combine a trip to Jamaica to see the folks with a visit to The Institute there and I could do some research on Port Royal, the wicked pirate city.'

Anna looked surprised, as only moments before he had spoken of Spain and now he was talking of a trip to Jamaica, but she knew her Dad's ways, so just nodded, fairly sure it wouldn't happen.

He drained his tea. ' The Institute's on East Street in Kingston, not far from Auntie Sarah's and I 'd love to learn more about our ancestors. We'll see. Anyway we'd better be going.'

They soon stepped out into Euston Road. Anna, in jeans and bomber jacket hardly felt the drizzle, but after a week in sunny Spain she watched her Dad pull up the collar of his waterproof jacket. They turned left and walked briskly toward King's Cross Underground station.

'I'll try the charts in the British Museum on Monday.'

They reached the Underground and hurried down the crowded steps. Her Dad gave her a hug. 'I'll collect you later from the rink and we'll go on to Jonathan's.' She saw the twinkle in his eye. 'By the way, how do you fancy Key West in Florida this Easter holiday?'

She just stared at him, puzzled. Did he mean it? School broke up yesterday so she was free.

'Jonathan's hired a salvage ship and we're going to try and locate the "Don Carlos". Bring a friend.'

'AMAZING Dad, I'll ask Jodie. When do we go?'

'Next weekend I think. I wasn't sure you'd want to come, as it's not exactly your sort of holiday, so I've been trying to get around to asking you. Anyway got to go now. See you later,' and he gave her another hug and hurried away, leaving her staring after him. She pulled her iPhone from her jacket pocket and quickly texted Jodie, ''c u at ice rink at 3 got news xx''.

Anna clung to the barrier and shivered, as Jodie skimmed around the rink, looking like a model in her fluffy pink jumper and ironed-on jeans. It was as though she had skated since birth. She sped towards Anna with her blonde hair flying and expertly turned her skate to brake. The ice flew up in a satisfying scrunch.

She took Anna's arm, 'Come on you can do it.' Anna finally let go of the barrier and hanging on to Jodie, with ankles caving, made a circuit, Jodie deftly steering her round the crowds. She smiled up at Jodie and they began another death-defying lap.

'How do you fancy a trip to the Caribbean this holiday?'

Jodie span around, lost the edge and went over on her backside, long legs thrust out in front of her. Anna burst out laughing. Then over Anna went and they both sat with wet backsides, giggling on the ice. Jodie pulled her phone from her jeans pocket and took a selfie of them both laughing at the camera.

Jodie pulled Anna to her feet. 'Are you serious?'

'Absolutely. My Dad's going to the Caribbean over

the holidays with Jonathan to help him search for this old Spanish ship. They've said I can come along and bring a friend. Jonathan's organised it all. It's for real.'

They skated around slowly, Anna clinging to Jodie's arm. 'That would be awesome Anna.'

' Dad talked about a salvage ship, a bit of an old crate I should think.'

'Yeah, but the Caribbean, sun, sand, guys.' She let go of Anna's arm, skated off at speed and performed a salko, effortlessly leaping and spinning in the air, tearing back and offering Anna her arm.

'We'll be based somewhere off Florida, near coral reefs, so make sure you pack your snorkeling gear.'

'This just gets better.'

They set off again dodging four children holding hands. Jodie skated backwards, bending her knees and gliding, pulling Anna along. 'Mum and Dad will be thrilled.' Her voice gave her away. Anna knew that they would happily pay to see the back of their daughter for a few weeks so that they could get on with their busy city lives.

'Fancy a hot chocolate Jodie?'

'Brilliant.'

'My ankles are killing me.'

'Those guys over there fancy you.'

'Me?'

'Yes you idiot you're beautiful.' She grabbed Anna's arm. 'Come on with a bit of luck they'll follow us.'

* * *

Anna stared around in wonder. She had never visited

the Professor's house in Notting Hill. Jonathan's large Victorian drawing room, with its high ceiling and cast iron fireplace, was laid out like a museum. Classical marble statues defended the corners and African masks guarded the walls. A glass cabinet stacked with fine blue and white Chinese porcelain stood opposite the fireplace. Anna studied several of the plates carefully.

'You like my crockery collection?' Jonathan stood beside her smiling brightly, even more like a child than her father. The pair had been friends since their university days at Cambridge. Jonathan always looked like he had spent the last hour playing rugby in his best suit, his remaining grey hair standing out in all directions.

'It was dated at Christies, the auction house, as 1630s, the Ming Dynasty. It came from a wreck in the Indian Ocean.'

'I love it. Mum started a collection the year before she died of that stupid cancer.'

'Well your mother would. She always had great taste.'

Anna smiled at him and nodded then wandered into the room across the hallway and could not take her eyes from a gold figurine of an eagle. Jonathan followed her and gave it to her to hold. 'Fine piece isn't it? Probably used in an Inca ritual to their gods. What do you think James?' Anna held it out to her Dad. It was cold and heavy with a primitive beauty.

He put on his reading glasses and studied it, turning it over in his long fingers. 'I think it's late Inca, probably early sixteenth century before the Spanish conquest. I can't be sure of course.'

Whatever it was Anna was sad to see it put back on the shelf to gather dust. Jonathan went off to the kitchen to make tea and she continued to stare at it. He soon returned with three mugs on a tray.

They sank into a leather couch in the bow window. 'To business. Well everything is ready for us to search for the wreck. We have the financial backing and I've hired a crew. The ship's a good old tub with space below for a control room and a separate lab to clean and store the finds. Tim, my new assistant, flies out tomorrow to set up the computer system. I go on Wednesday to equip the lab. Are you bringing a friend Anna?'

'Yes please. My best friend, Jodie.'

'The more the merrier.' His smile creased his whole face, so that he looked like an old sea captain from picture books. 'We have eye witness reports from local divers that there is something down there, about a mile or so off Key West. They say it's all broken up. I think it's the "Don Carlos", but I would love more documentation to prove it. All we have is the one letter written by the Spanish priest.' He looked at James hopefully.

James shook his head. 'No luck at the moment.'

'Keep up the good work. In the meantime I'll inform the local police of the dates we're on site. I've arranged a license from the US government. There are a lot of sharks out there and they are not all of the fish variety.'

Anna's Dad left the room only to reappear, grinning like a schoolboy, with a plate of cream cakes. Anna tucked into a chocolate éclair. He must have been to the supermarket with Jonathan. He never took a list like

Mum used to do and bought the craziest things. The cakes were one of his better ideas.

'So what's this you have to show me then Dad? You've not bought another DVD of some rock group of your youth?'

'No, but if you want…'

'No thanks Dad.'

She finished her éclair, licked her fingers of chocolate and followed as he beckoned her into Jonathan's dining room. On the table stood a large wooden model of an old ship with four masts and square canvas sails. It was exquisite.

She rushed over to the table as her Dad explained.

'Jonathan made it. Do tell us about it.'

Jonathan walked around his model, looking at it critically, as if he would like to improve it. 'It's a seventeenth century Spanish galleon. It would have been in the convoy taking treasure back from Cartagena in Colombia to Spain. With a good wind the voyage would have taken about two months.'

Anna stared in wonder at the beautiful ship, richly carved and painted in red and gold, canvas sails about to catch the wind. The gun ports stood hinged open with the cannon ready to fire.

'The ship's correct in every detail, as far as is possible with current knowledge from wreck sites and contemporary written records: five hundred tons with an armament of fifty four cannon and two swivel guns, a keel length of thirty metres and a beam of eleven metres. In other words she is a very big ship and not very manoeuvrable. The hardest part was carving all the Spanish sailors and soldiers.' Jonathan said more but she no longer heard him.

Anna picked up a sailor to find him half the size of her little finger. In her imagination she had drunk a potion like Alice in "Alice in Wonderland" and shrunk to explore the galleon.

She climbed down a step ladder from the weather deck on to the main deck and saw the gunners loading the heavy carriage guns. She passed the helmsman steering the ship with a long pole, then climbed down the ladder on to the orlop deck. Here the men relaxed, one playing a lute, others eating meat from wooden bowls. She wandered into the galley and a fire burned fiercely in the brick furnace, as the cook stirred a copper cauldron.

She clambered down into the lower hold, where rats scuttled across the barrels and there was the treasure! Hordes of silver bars were stacked amongst the rock ballast, and they shone like the moon on water and she smiled at her Dad in wonder. It was like a floating safe deposit vault. He pointed to the many chests in the hold above and told her everyone was full to the brim with gold or silver coins and the crates with gold bars.

He gave her a hug. 'So we fly from Heathrow to Miami next weekend, then down to the Keys. You'll love it there. We can swim and snorkel, visit the Treasure Museum housing the finds from the Spanish galleon, the "Atocha". It sank off the Keys in 1622 and a treasure hunter, Mel Fisher, found her and brought up a haul of gold and silver bars and jewellery. It will be an inspiration to us, but I hope our methods will be more scientific.'

Anna hardly heard him now as she punched the air and jumped around the room, WOW the Caribbean!

'I'll draw you a map of the route the Spanish treasure fleet took with the Florida Keys clearly marked.'

'Thanks Dad. I can't wait to go.'

CHAPTER 5

April 2013, Off Key West, Florida, USA

Whoops of joy came from the salvage ship, "Seeker", as the team peered at the sonar trace on the computer screen. For two days now there had been nothing to see as they towed the side-scan sonar along behind the ship, hoping it would pick up the wreck as a narrow mound on the sea bed. Jonathan called it "mowing the lawn". Anna tugged at her Dad's sleeve and he grinned at her, crossing his fingers.

There was something solid down there. Jonathan clapped his hands together, then as the ship cruised on he watched the screen in amazement, 'Another reading. Can there be two wrecks at such a short distance?' He turned to Captain Tomkins, 'What do you think Charlie?'

'This area's ankle deep in wrecks so I don't know how you missed 'em. Could be a wreck ourselves if the weather turns nasty. It changes in the twinkle of an eye round here.'

Jonathan looked at Charlie's melancholy face, into his watery eyes; no twinkle there. 'Well thanks Charlie. Would you cut the engines?'

'Sure thing', and the old sea captain took up the handset and called the bridge. 'Harry shut her off will you and drop the anchor. They think they've found something.' The engines, cranking and grinding in complaint, finally fell silent.

'Tim, let's try the maggy.' Jonathan's young assistant adjusted his glasses and slid his chair from the sonar to the adjacent screen.

Anna pulled up the strap on her green bikini top, 'What on earth's a maggy?'

'It's a magnetometer. It takes readings every metre from where it's trailed along the sea bed. Look. It's indicating something. Do you see the red against the black?'

Anna could only make out red blobs, but picked up on the general excitement.

Jonathan rubbed his hands together in delight. 'First we'll clear the area of sand and see what we're doing. Charlie start the propwash up.'

Minutes later Anna heard a whirring sound, like a swarm of buzzing bees, and the propwash covering the ship's propeller directed a jet of water at the seabed, clearing the area of sand and silt. Jonathan turned to his team of divers. 'Time for the first dive.' He looked thoughtful now. 'If this is the wreck it is also a grave site, so we will hold a short service this evening if you are in agreement.'

Everybody nodded.

'Now to work. Alysia you set up the airlift and keep the site clear of sand.'

'Right you are.'

Anna had got to know all the divers in the past few days. She knew Alysia had no time for research and she was bounding up the steps to the deck two at a time. Jonathan turned to a young red-haired man at the back of the group. 'Joe, you take the camera and get us an overview of the site.'

Joe crossed the room and picked up the heavy underwater camera.

'Steve and Pete, get ready to measure and map.' Steve was a bouncer in a night club and a man of few words. He simply nodded. Anna found Pete very serious and a mine of information on shipping, which could become tedious. 'Kirsty you photograph all and everything and Jason start on the drawings.' Kirsty was a photojournalist, keen and professional, a camera always strung around her neck. Jason was tall and thin and strutted across the room like a heron to collect his waterproof paper and board. Anna heard them agreeing that it was too warm for wet suits, which would mean less kitting up. She must learn to Scuba dive.

Within half an hour the divers were back on board towelling themselves down. Joe set them all off laughing, making fun of Pete's fluorescent green Bermuda shorts. 'If we ever got lost at sea Pete we'll just hang your shorts out. No need for GPS.' He turned his attention to Jason's long sunburnt legs. 'Much more sun Jason and the lady flamingos will be after you.' They all went below to change, laughing.

Shortly all of them met in the control room again. Jonathan loaded Joe's footage into the laptop and the chatter and laughter died away. Anna watched the screen as the divers swam along the coral reef. A ray fish swam away looking dark and mysterious, seeming to fly like a Stealth fighter plane.

Alysia cleared the white sand with the airlift. It was

like a giant vacuum cleaner and swirls of sand flew up like talcum powder shaken on after a bath. Anna gripped her Dad's arm as she saw the ribbed framework of the hull, laying on its side like the skeleton of a giant whale. Part of the keel lay snapped like a twig. Fish swam in and out exploring, as though it were an underwater cave. Anna jigged with excitement, praying it was the "Don Carlos."

Steve and Pete swam across the site hammering in stakes and tying PVC ropes in a grid to map the timbers. Their air bubbles rose rhythmically to the surface, their weightless bodies soothing to watch. Jason crouched on the sea bed sketching a clay pipe as it lay half buried in the sand. Jonathan pointed at the screen excitedly, 'That reef there might not be a reef at all, but more of the hull covered in corals and sponges.'

Her father gave her a hug. 'Water preserves wood, leather and even food and the sand has covered the timbers keeping out the oxygen which speeds up the decay . It's like a time capsule down there. Once we take a sample of the timber we can send it to the lab back in England for dendrochronology dating. The rings on the timber will be counted and compared with other dated samples and that will give the age of the tree when it was felled and we will know roughly when the ship was built.'

Jonathan pointed at the screen and grew excited again. 'That looks like a cannon.' Anna looked hard at the lump of rock to which he pointed. 'If we can lift that and send it back to the university lab for X-ray and cleaning we should find the name of the cannon works and hopefully a date engraved on the barrel.

Anna stared harder but still saw a lump of old rock, except it was long and very roughly cylindrical.

'The name of the founder would give us the century, but a date would be fantastic. We'll know that if the cannon was made in say 1660 that the ship can be no later than that date.' He paused for breath, rubbing his chin. 'We need to be careful though because the engraving may be the weight of the gun not the date.'

Anna looked at Jonathan in amazement then more closely at the long shape. 'It doesn't look anything like a cannon.'

Her Dad grinned. 'It's covered in concretions, a crusty coating of minerals and sand. The conservationists back home will drill it away very carefully, like a dentist removing plaque from teeth. It's probably made of cast iron, as bronze was being used less by the mid seventeenth century.' He turned to Jonathan. 'But can we lift it?'

'We've got airbags to float it to the surface and lifting gear to get it on deck, but it will be tricky. It'll probably weigh half a ton.' He stared hard at the screen. 'What we really need to do is find the ship's bell. It will give the name of the ship and the date it was built, conclusive evidence that we have found the "Don Carlos". That would be a find, but when you think the scatter from the site could be up to twelve kilometres, we've got quite a search on our hands. Plus the fact we may well have another wreck down there.'

Anna peered at the screen looking for anything that might look like a bell, but all she could see were the divers near the reef, shoals of brightly coloured fish and the timbers.

She went in search of Jodie and found her in their cabin painting her nails. She looked up and smiled, 'I've had a lovely sleep. 'Shall we go for a swim when my nails have dried?'

'Excellent.'

'I'm having a great time Anna.' She stood up and tied a silk sarong around her pink bikini. 'We could go snorkeling?'

'Could do. What I should really love is to go deeper. I should love to learn to Scuba dive so that we could visit the wreck site.'

'What does that mean?'

'SCUBA stands for Self-Contained, Underwater Breathing Apparatus. Basically you carry your own supply of compressed air in a cylinder on your back, so you can dive as long as the air holds out.'

'Sounds fun. Ask your Dad.' She peered at her purple nails. 'I've got the money. Mum and Dad gave me loads. Mum says the shopping's great in Key West, designer, and the restaurants are good, especially for shrimp dishes. Couldn't wait to see me off.' She laughed, twirling strands of long blonde hair around her finger. 'Have they found some more old wood?'

'They think they might have found one of the cannon.'

'Oh right, only that anorak, Pete, went on and on this morning about how they built old ships. I thought I was going to die. I could hardly eat my muesli.'

'Come on let's go up on deck for some sun.'

Jodie grabbed the sun tan oil and they raced up the steps into the sparkling light and the deep blue Caribbean Sea.

Anna saw her Dad talking to Captain Tomkins and as he turned to walk towards her she raced up to him. 'Dad, can Jodie and I take diving lessons at Key West because we want to be close to the fishes and the wreck?'

'I don't see why not as long as you do exactly as you're told. Diving can be a very dangerous game, but I think it only takes three or four days here to get a certificate.'

Anna hugged him and ran to tell Jodie.

Her Dad called after her, 'I'll arrange some lessons when we go into Key West this evening. As for diving on the wreck you'll have to talk to the diving team about that.'

Night fell with hardly a drop in temperature. Anna sat on the deck reading a novel, "Coram Boy", under the lights from the bridge. Jodie slept below in their cabin. After the London drizzle, Anna revelled in the warm evening air. She looked up from her book as a frigate bird glided on the air current. He looked so powerful, with a large wing span and long, hooked beak.

It was peaceful. Everyone had gone off in the small motor boat to Key West, except for Tim, who rarely left the computer. The divers were heading for 'a big night' as Kirsty put it, at "Sloppy Joe's" bar.

The ship rocked gently at anchor, well away from the dangerous reefs which had seen so many ships wrecked over the years. She put down her book. It was hard to believe on an evening like this that vicious storms and hurricanes could blow in unexpectedly from the west. She looked up at the stars and tried to remember what her Dad had told her about the different constellations. Was that Orion up there?

She heard the roar of a motor boat engine and saw lights in the distance on the water. It drew alongside the "Seekers" and the engine spluttered out.

'Hello there.' A young man in a crumpled cream suit stood on the prow waving to her, illuminated by the light shining from the cabin. His partner waved happily and called up in a refined English accent. 'We're out of fuel to get back to port.' Do you have a spare can? We'll return it full of course.'

Anna called back, 'Hold on and I'll go and find some.' She climbed down the steps to the control room and asked Tim where the fuel was stored. It was a heavy can so Tim followed her up on deck with it. She stared in horror at the four masked men in black on the deck, only a few paces away.

A small man pointed a revolver at them and the three behind towered over him and were built like boxers. The young couple were nowhere to be seen. 'Now if you just do as we say nobody get hurt.' He had a slight accent. Was it Italian, Spanish? She wasn't sure. 'We want the plans of the wreck site, laptops, documents.' He pointed the gun at Tim and forced him down into the control room. 'I want everything or she dies.' As he went below, following Tim, one man followed and the other two produced revolvers and pointed them at Anna. She tried not to show her fear and prayed Jodie would wake soon and raise the alarm. She dared not call her and involve her in this nightmare.

All waited until Tim reappeared and handed over papers and a laptop, his hands shaking. The man with the accent pointed the gun at Tim's head. 'Is that everything? What about finds?'

'No finds yet.'

One of the men forced Tim down on the decking, tied his feet and hands and gagged him.

'Bring the girl as hostage.'

Anna screamed 'No.'

'Oh yes. You'll be our bargaining counter.' He signalled to the thugs with the revolvers and they bundled Anna into the motor boat.

CHAPTER 6

Anna awoke to daylight and found herself in a log cabin, an air-conditioning fan whirring on the ceiling. Rubbing her eyes she tried to think where she was, her head pounding. She suspected she had been drugged. One of the thugs from the speedboat sat next to the door, a gun laid across his huge thighs and reality flooded over her.

The only window, which was opposite her, was barred. She pulled herself up on the divan bed to discover her whole body ached. All she could see was a gravel drive, then forest, thick and dark, but she heard the sea lapping the shore. A small green lizard slithered across the wooden flooring.

She wanted to cry but her words came out defiant. 'You'll never get away with this. The Florida police will be looking for me right now.'

The man shrugged. He was Afro-Caribbean, like herself, but his neck was the size of her waist. He picked up a bag of chocolate doughnuts from the table next to him and slowly ate. 'Wanna doughnut?'

'No thank you.' She tried a little girl's voice.' I just want to go back to my Daddy. He'll be really worried.'

This didn't work. He didn't flicker a muscle.

'Where are we?'

He shrugged.

'Are we still in Florida?'

He ignored her.

She looked around the room trying to find some clue that would tell her where she was, but there was nothing. The log walls were bare. The pine dining table in the centre of the room stood empty, four chairs neatly tucked underneath. She checked her watch; eleven o'clock. Had she been here longer than one night? The television on the wall opposite the bed was switched off.

'Can I watch TV?'

He picked up the remote control, pointed it at the television then flicked through the channels. He stopped at "The Simpsons". If only she could be as smart as Lisa and find her way out of this mess.

Doughnut roared with laughter and was soon engrossed, grunting and smirking, stuffing in more doughnuts. As the show finished she got off the divan slowly and fetched the remote control. He watched her every move. 'Can I change the channel?'

No response, so she desperately searched for the news channels she usually avoided. He paid no attention. She found CNN and soon discovered that a woman in Miami had won two million pounds on the lottery and a thirteen year old boy had been arrested for drug smuggling on Miami Beach. They must be somewhere near Miami for sure.

Above the whine of the woman news presenter she heard footsteps scrunching on the gravel and turned off the television. Doughnut stood up stuffing the last doughnut in his mouth.

The door opened and a small man walked in carrying a briefcase. He was deeply tanned and wore a green linen suit and highly polished brown shoes. Unlike Doughnut the look he gave frightened her. His eyes were almost black and strangely piercing. He was followed by three burly white men all wearing various shades of grey suits.

They all ignored her and sat down at the dining table leaving Doughnut on guard. The small man took papers from his case and spread them out on the table, his fingers loaded with gold jewellery. He lit a fat cigar and choked the room with smoke.

'Here is the wreck of the "Don Carlos." Anna recognised the foreign voice. As she guessed, it was the masked man from the motor boat and the others must be his men with the revolvers. He stubbed his short finger down on the map and looking up, smiled thinly at her, knowing very well she was listening to every word. 'Because we have her the archaeologists won't go near the site for fear she will be harmed and nor will the police. I've sent word that if we are stopped on the site she dies.'

He puffed on his cigar. 'So gentlemen, the wreck is ours. The ship sank with silver ingots aboard and chests full of gold coins and Colombian emeralds. Justin found the inventory in a Seville archive.'

All three bodyguards looked blank.

'It's a list of what was on the ship. Old documents are kept in an archive.'

They all nodded.

He pulled a crumpled parchment from his jacket pocket. Anna could not believe her eyes. She had seen her father carefully pull on white gloves before handling old manuscripts. He spread it out on the table like a shopping list and studied it. He was Spanish; that was the slight accent.

Anna remembered what her father had said. He had searched for the inventory of the ship in Seville and had not found it. The man he called Justin must have got there first and stolen it.

'We hire a team of top divers and offer them a share of the haul.' He narrowed his eyes, 'Not a large share.'

The men laughed.

'We fetch up the gold and jewels and sail away into the sunset.' He turned to Anna and sneered, 'We don't have a lot of time for your Daddy's toothbrush methods.'

The thugs roared with laughter and one of them used a pretend toothbrush to carefully scrub at the gold signet ring biting into his little finger.

The small man sat back and puffed on his cigar. 'This is much better than the rich men's yachts we usually prey on in the Caribbean.' He looked at Anna again. 'My name is Rodrigo,' and he gestured at the others. 'These men are my friends.' All of them sat immobile, arms crossed. 'You will come to no harm if you do as I say and if you're a good girl you'll soon go home to Daddy.'

Anna had never felt so angry and frustrated. They were modern day pirates and she guessed Rodrigo was not his real name, but she masked her feelings and pretended to cry. *They would spoil the wreck site just to get gold which belonged to the US government; gold that would help pay for a museum to house any finds and tell archaeologists so much about the seventeenth century world. She was thinking like her Dad!*

'Can you Scuba dive?' he asked her suddenly.

She used the voice needed with the maths teacher when she was late with her homework. 'No, but if I have diving lessons and get my certificate perhaps I could help you. Would you give me a share of the gold, a ring or something? I think I saw a big chest in the sand.'

They all stared at her. 'Sure little girl. You can have a ring if you help the divers find the big chest. It's usually kept in the back of the ship, near the Captain's cabin. You can have a necklace too, but what would your Daddy say?'

His voice was so patronising Anna thought she would be sick. She pouted her lips and looked sullen. 'I don't care what he says because he never lets me do what I want.' She smiled around at them and called to Doughnut. 'Can I have a chocolate doughnut or have you eaten them all?'

The thugs laughed and Rodrigo took his mobile from his inside pocket and arranged diving lessons for her from 'people who wouldn't talk.' They would start that afternoon and would continue for the next few days.

The door opened once more and in strolled the Englishman from the motor boat. He wore the same crumpled suit. The sun-tanned woman who had waved to her so cheerily followed him. She now wore a red sundress and twirled her sunglasses. It was worth noting everything to inform the police if she ever got out of this hut. They both ignored her. He spoke in an upper class English accent. 'The inventory is useful to you then Rodrigo? Excellent. It took a lot of work to steal that from the archives. When do I get my cut?'

Rodrigo looked up. 'Be patient Justin, soon enough,' and he returned to his shopping list of gold and silver.

* * *

A few days later Rodrigo's white speedboat raced towards the wreck site, a plume of sea spray shooting out behind. Anna sat in her wetsuit, near the stern, watching the white surf as the boat skimmed the choppy sea like a bouncing bomb. Doughnut, at the wheel, shouted to Rodrigo, 'Thirty knots Boss.' The speed across the water was terrific. It was like being in a James Bond film, except the sky wasn't Technicolor blue, but threateningly black.

As they approached the wreck site and slowed down Anna saw that "Seeker" was not there. Rodrigo sat next to Doughnut on the white leather seat looking out over the grey sea. The other three thugs sat behind, machine guns ready waiting for Rodrigo to give them instructions whilst the three divers pulled on their flippers and oxygen tanks.

Anna's heart pounded as a diver helped her strap the air cylinder to her back. The instructor who taught her in the sea near the log cabin told her she was a natural diver and right now she needed to believe that. It was true she felt happy underwater, calm and relaxed, in spite of only a few days training.

She joined the other three as they thrust knives into their belts. She asked the diver nearest her, 'Have you ever been attacked by a shark?'

He laughed. 'Knives are useful against sharks, but they don't usually go for us. We use them to fend off other wreck divers; far more dangerous than sharks.'

They all put on their face masks and one of them picked up a metal detector. They plunged backwards off the side of the boat into the water and Anna followed them.

She swam down deeper and deeper, kicking her flippers and keeping her arms close to her body. Her instructor had called it 'streamlining.' She adjusted her face mask to trap air. As she reached the reef she swam on in wonder at its teeming life of multi-coloured corals, some like fans wafting in the current, cooling the water. She passed a shoal of blue and rainbow parrotfish gnawing at the coral with their beak-like mouths. Then she saw a seahorse, its tail curled around the seaweed for anchorage.

Now the divers followed, bubbles of used air floating up to the surface from each of them. One swept the sand with the metal detector searching for the ingots and a black sea snake swam out and away. She swam over the timbers of the ship that until now she had only seen on the computer screen, touched them, touched history. She found what they had thought to be the cannon and smoothed the sand from the barnacles.

The divers followed her as she swam on pretending to search for the chest. Her heart leapt with fear as she saw a man's chubby hand on the edge of the reef. As she drew closer she breathed a sigh of relief to find it was the soft coral, dead man's fingers and her heart rate slowly returned to normal.

She spotted an anchor shape encrusted in rock and tried hard to remember its position from the cannon to tell her Dad. This must be the stern of the ship. The divers suddenly stopped and began to pick silver coins, pieces of eight, from the sand, like greedy boys with sweets, searching wildly in the sand for more.

Anna disappeared behind the reef and swam away. She quickly looked at her watch; fifteen more minutes of air. Swimming up towards the light she finally plunged through the surface and ripped off her air mask and like a sleek seal, tasted the salt. Untying the cylinder, she let it sink to the soft seabed.

There was no sign of them yet. Replacing the mask to protect her eyes, she struck out for the shore with a fast crawl. She kept her head down, arms sweeping the water aside, kicking with her flippers, as the swimming teacher had drummed into the class in PE. Then she had only played at pirates in the school pool. Here she knew she was at least a mile from shore. By controlling her breathing she set a steady rhythm. The rain began to pelt down, the sea grew choppier and Anna swam for her life.

CHAPTER 7

Port Royal, Jamaica, May 1668

Anika's mother had an African saying that when the croaking lizard sang it was a sign that rain would soon come. The gecko had sung and the rain beat on the pantiled roof of their house like war drums. It had rained all night and morning and looked set to continue. Anika ate the last slice of refreshing mango and licked her fingers. She decided to tell her fears, bottled up for too long and gnawing at her stomach.

Crossing the stone flags to where her mother lay, worn and frail in her hammock, Anika spoke all in a rush, in her mother's Ashanti. 'Mama I'm frightened. I think that soon there will be sugar plantations everywhere on Jamaica and that I will be forced to work as a slave as you did in Barbados.' There, it was said.

She stared out of the slatted window on to the cobbled street at the rain splashing and dancing. Her dream of finding the wrecks of "Don Carlos" and " Black Lady" seemed as impossible as flying away like a frigate bird, but she would never give up a dream.

She turned to see her mother smiling at her. She looked much older than her thirty years and Anika felt guilty for saying anything. *Why had her Mama's tribe sold her as a slave to the English? The chief had sold her for twenty manillas; copper bracelets. Her beautiful mother sold for bracelets.* Anger boiled up inside her and she strode over to the hearth and seizing a coconut and cleaver hacked through the husk, the sweet smell of the milk pungent in the small room.

Her mother raised herself on her bony elbow and took the coconut shell to drink. She spoke slowly in a reed thin voice. 'Governor Modyford will import slaves from Africa, but much land will need to be cleared and many slaves brought. It will take time and a great deal of money to buy the machinery and the slaves. The governor won't be able to raise it at the moment after fighting the Dutch and the French.' She smiled and took Anika's hand. 'You will be safe.'

Anika was not comforted by her mother's kind words as she thought of all those Africans who would be enslaved. Her thoughts ran away with her. *There were already some plantations on the south coast. She was a mulatto, or as the English called her, mixed race; so why not her? If she did escape the plantations what about her children and their children? She did not want them to grow up as slaves on a sugar plantation, cutting cane in the fierce heat, working the machinery .She wanted them to be free.*

She wanted to tell them stories about the cunning spiderman Anancy, as her mother had told her, to teach them to swim and dive and fish. No human being should be enslaved to another. What right had they?

She stood up and waved away the mosquitoes swarming around the water cask. She had painted the room blue to keep away the flies and mosquitoes, but still they came. It was time to prepare the meal as her mother would not have the strength whilst she and Antonio were out in the boat. He would be in the

"King's Arms" around the corner most of the day. She climbed the ladder to the small room above and fetched her favourite knife from the oak chest beside her hammock.

Pumping hard on the bellows at the hearth, she set the fire to burn, washed and gutted the swordfish at the old table in the corner and threw the fillets in the pot, then poured in the snowy coconut milk.

She chopped the peppers angrily imagining her mother crammed in a ship's hold with the other negro slaves brought from Guinea; chained to another woman by the ankle, unable to move. *Why should she cut sugar cane all day so that English ladies might have sugar in their new drink, tea?*

As she peeled and chopped the ginger her mother began to talk. 'I ran away from Barbados and stowed in an English merchant ship heading for Port Royal. The ship was called "Intrepid". I married your Papa here at St Peter's church. He had found his way to Jamaica in 1655 after the English colony was founded there that year. He was kind and gentle, not like the Englishmen I knew.'

Her mother had never spoken of all this before.

'He started cattle ranching. The Spanish conquest in the early 1500s had wiped out the native Arawak Indians, by harsh treatment and European diseases. All that was left of them was their cattle and pigs in the scrub and forest. Those people called this island "Xaymaca", land of woods and water, which is how it got its name.

'But his heart was not in farming and he became a fisherman here. It was the only major town. It still is. We moved into this house and stayed.'

She sipped her coconut milk. 'As the years went by all the driftwood seemed to end up here in Port Royal, beggars, criminals, those without work. Some were sent out from England to the colony as servants to masters they may not leave for seven years. There were buccaneers, merchants and mariners.' She sat up slightly and caught her breath.

'You were born the following year, 29 March 1656 and Daniel was born two years later. We named you Anika in remembrance of your Papa's Russian ancestors. You were five when your Papa died. The heat didn't suit him Anika. Many of his white friends died of the fever too.' She settled back, tired of her memories. 'He was a good man.' She closed her eyes and rested. Anika remembered him clutching her hand, lying there in his hammock, soaked in sweat and shaking, his body racked with pain.

Her mother stirred slightly and Anika smiled across at her. 'Mama. I've put in plenty of ginger, just the way you like it,' and she dipped the ladle into the pot and tasted it. She hung the pot high on the rack over the hearth fire and the room filled with wood smoke. The rain continued to rattle on the roof.

Someone hammered on the door and Anika called for them to come in, speaking English.

'Diego. What are you doing here?'

'I have a boat. I have a boat.' He jigged around like a demon, a puddle of rain water forming at his feet. 'My uncle. He pirate. He die and he leave the boat and all his charts to me. She is new Anika, only built a few months ago.' He hugged Anika and danced her round the room, until she held him at arm's length, breathless.

'He taught me to sail, to read the charts, everythin', but I keep quiet on the pirate ship because I no want to 'elp them. I jus stir my stew.' He took Anika by the arm. 'Come see, come see.'

Her mother smiled and waved them away, so Anika grabbed her cloak from the back of the door and kissed her mother. 'I'll be back very soon. The meal is cooking,' and she and Diego raced out into the street. They hurried on into the smelly market square, awash with the rain, and grabbed fronded banana leaves from a fruit stall and held them over their heads.

He rushed her down to the harbour where they passed many pirate ships. Judging from the snatches of conversation they had just returned from a raid on French shipping. There were also Royal Navy men- of- war, bristling with cannon, the officers in blue uniforms with gold braid and buttons shouting orders to the weather-beaten crew.

Diego's eyes shone and he pointed proudly, 'There is my beautiful boat.'

He pointed at a new ketch, two- masted with a slim hull for speed through the water and a long bowsprit for the latest triangular sails. In bold black letters on her hull she read "Pearl." The ketch is named for you. In England they say pearls of wisdom and that is you, because you think hard about everything and also you dive for the pearls.' She threw her arms around him and planted a kiss on his cheek. He flushed and hurried her on.

'Come.' He took her aboard, showing her the fine woodwork and she breathed in tar from the newly caulked decking. He took her down to the galley. 'Say you be my cook, then you never have to work for Antonio.'

Anika was taken aback. *Not work for Antonio? What would he say?*

'Do no worry. We make plenty money trading to give to Antonio and he will be happy. I pay you to be cook and you share in profits.'

Anika knew she wanted nothing to do with piracy. *What about Mama?*

He read her thoughts. 'We trade logwood, bananas. Maybe some hides. We bring food and money to your Mama and maybe she come with us sometimes.'

She smiled and could not believe her good fortune. Just an hour ago her future had looked so bleak.

Diego danced her about the weather deck, jigging in the puddles.

'Hey Diego.' Her stomach tightened at the sound of his voice. 'What you doin' on your uncle's boat?' 'Antonio stood on the wharf in the rain, swaying slightly, a tankard in his hand.

Diego told Antonio of his plans for Anika.

Antonio struggled aboard and took her roughly by the arm. 'She stays with me.' He pulled out his dagger and glaring into her eyes put the knife to her throat, 'You no want anything happen to your Mama do you?'

Anika hung her head as she left the boat. Antonio stared down at her. 'You goin' to be busy girl. You cook now Diego gone and you dive.'

They returned to the house and he kicked open the door. 'I need tobacco so go to market and be quick.'

As night fell Antonio snored in his hammock, an empty tankard thrown to the floor. Her mother slept soundly.

Anika threw her cloak around her and crept out of the house into the starry night. At last the rain had stopped.

Port Royal never slept. From every inn she passed, and there were many, came music and singing, shrieks of laughter and from some the crash of furniture and angry voices as fights broke out. Father Thomas, from her church, called it 'the wickedest place in Christendom', where taverns jostled with churches, synagogues and mosques. It was a mad, whirling, swirling place.

The streets were jammed with people, speaking all languages. Jewels glinted in the lantern light off velvet gowns and silk suits. She fought her way through tethered horses, neighing and stomping, and a file of donkeys loaded with panniers of tobacco leaves. A woman's musky perfume nearly choked her as she passed the warehouses of English merchants, their iron gates guarded by armed men. Antonio said they overflowed with goods bought from the pirates; precious silks and brocades, fabulous jewels and Chinese porcelain, tobacco and sugar; all waiting to be shipped to Europe in English ships.

She ducked down an unlit alleyway and the brick houses of three and four storeys seemed to topple in on her. Covering her mouth against the stench of dung, she stopped at a noisy tavern, "The Black Dog", and pushed open the heavy door. The coarse smell of tobacco and the smoke clung to the low ceiling and made her cough. She searched through the haze for Stephen but could not see him, but spotted the portly merchant who now owned this so-called tippling house. It seemed to Anika these men had drunk far more than a small tipple.

He lurched across the room making for the piss pots in the corner. Since Captain Jameson's death Stephen had worked for him as a manservant. Then she saw Stephen taking a jug of rum to a table in the corner and she crossed the room, aware of the many eyes upon her.

He placed the jug in the middle of the excited poker players. She tapped him lightly on the shoulder and as he turned a smile lit up his face. Two weeks had passed since she had last seen him and now she knew how much she had missed him. They sat on a trestle bench and she told him all that had happened.

An hour later, when most of the revellers lay blind drunk in the straw on the floor and rats gnawed at the candle stubs, she took his hand and led him down to Diego's boat in the harbour. They climbed aboard and found Diego asleep in his cabin. Anika shook him awake.

She took them both by the hands and said, 'This is my plan....'

CHAPTER 8

A week later, as night fell, Antonio left their house for "The King's Arms". He would probably be gone all night because he was celebrating. On three separate dives off the coast of Panama Anika had found a pearl each time. She took them from the tankard on the shelf over the hearth, nestled them in the purse hung at her waist and drew the leather thongs tight.

Anika stood in the doorway and watched him wander down the moonlit street and around the corner. She quickly shut the door and she and her mother packed their few belongings in a sack. 'You are right Anika. I am as much a slave here with Antonio as I was on the plantation. It's time to go.' She paused to catch her breath. ' He should have let you work for Diego. He has no claim on you because I never married him. He is your stepfather only in name.'

Anika saw her mother tiring quickly. 'Sit down Mama. I'll do this. You'll need your strength.' The crickets chirruped outside as if in agreement.

Her mother sat down gratefully on the bench by the hearth and smiled across at Anika. 'There's an old Caribbean saying about the storms around the islands here and when you should begin a sea voyage, and it goes like this:

June too soon
July stand by

August come they must
September, remember
October all over.
We set sail in May, so good fortune attend us all!'

Anika rushed over and hugged her mother, so happy to be taking her away at last. She kissed her, hurriedly tied up the sack and blew out the candles. Taking her mother's arm they left the house and struggled through the crowded streets into the lantern-lit harbour.

Her mother looked away in horror as chains of African slaves linked by neck irons were unloaded from the slaving ship like cattle; manacles at their ankles rattling as they shuffled forward, half-dead from the cruel journey. They closed their eyes against the moonlight after the pitch darkness of the ship's hold. Tears sprang to Anika's eyes as one of the slavers whipped on a stumbling woman who stretched out her thin arm to a man in the chain of male slaves.

Anika rushed up to the English slave driver and screamed at him to stop. He hit her viciously across the face so that she nearly fell. 'I don't want mulattos; you ain't got the strength, or you'd join 'em.'

Her Mama pulled her away so forcefully Anika's wrist stung. She stared back at the cones of sugar waiting to be loaded and prayed this slave trade would not be Jamaica's future, feeling her people's pain.

Reaching Diego's ketch they met Stephen as arranged. He helped her mother aboard and Diego gave her the second cabin. 'This your new home.' It was as large as the ground floor room in their house and smelt of polished oak. He wore a broad-brimmed hat with an ostrich feather and swept this off, bowing low. A beautiful smile spread across her mother's face and Anika could have leapt for joy.

There were four other crewmen, survivors from "Black Lady"; Sean Murphy, the fiddler, the Scottish brothers, Robbie and Jimmy McDougal and the ex-navy gunner, Sam. They had become a tight crew as they sailed the Spanish salvage ship back to Port Royal and turned their backs on piracy.

The ketch sailed out of Port Royal on the dawn tide. Diego told the crew he had set a course for East Florida and a huge cheer went up when he told them of Anika's plan. They would be searching for the wrecks of the "Don Carlos" and "Black Lady". They were well provisioned: freshly caught blue and white marlin and a few snapper for the next day and salted beef and tuna to carry them over the Caribbean. Sweet potatoes and mangoes and bunches of bananas lay piled up in the galley and the chickens in the coop would provide eggs. The square sail on the mainmast raised and billowed in the following wind.

The crew soon began their usual wrangling as to who had suffered most at the hands of the First Officer, Gibbons.

Sam polished one of the four iron swivel guns mounted on the rails. 'He had me polishin' the cannon 'til me face shone in 'em. Then he'd come up, hands behind his back like some fancy navy officer and tell me to start on the swivels.'

Robbie coiled the rope and shook his head. 'He was a mean man, that he was. He had me flogged for "starin' at him." But Jameson was worse. He could change like the wind in the heather, one minute all jokes and smiles, the next murderous.'

Murphy told the story of how he had been forced to climb the rigging at great speed by Gibbons, 'Fearin' fer me life, as usual, bein no nat'ral sailor, and I seen Captain Jameson kill Gibbons. He was talkin' to 'im and then he just pulled his dagger and stabbed him through the heart, as God is me witness.'

They sailed with a stiff breeze all day and night. As dawn broke the new crew members slept and watched and watched and slept according to their turn. These were dangerous waters.

As the sun arose Anika lit a wood fire in the brick furnace and fetching the bellows pumped it with air until it burnt brightly. She had a hungry crew to feed. She hung the copper cauldron to boil and hurried up to the main deck to haul in the net from the stern. *Please let there be plenty of fish.* There were, including a tuna a yard long, enough for everyone. The rest she would use tomorrow or salt. Soon they joined the red peppers and sweet potatoes in the pot. The smell of ginger and coriander made mouths water. Diego passed the galley and grinned at her knowing he would never be asked to cook fish stew again.

The crew sat on the deck eating hungrily as the heat rose and grew fiercer. Sweat poured from Stephen's body, his skin red with sunburn. Anika fetched gourds of water and he thanked her and drank thirstily. 'I shall never get used to the heat of the Caribbean. Look at you, as cool as the dolphins.'

Anika smiled, 'I'll be back in a minute,' and hurried

down to the galley to fetch the aloe vera cream her mother had made as a protection against the sun. She smoothed the sweet-smelling cream on his back and shoulders, then sipped her drink and looked out over the turquoise water. The sea fascinated her; its moods, its colours, its secrets. As she stared out she saw a flying fish leap out of the water, its large fins spread as wings.

'This heat reminds me of a terrible fire Anika, in London. It was September 1666 and I was twelve.'

She turned to him interested as he rarely spoke of his life in England.

'The almanac writers prophesied a fire as a judgment from God on the sins of London and they turned out to be right.

'It started in a baker's shop in Pudding Lane, just around the corner from my family's house. I slept in the attic with Will, the apprentice, and awoke in the middle of the night to the smell of burning. I put my head out of the window and could see flames and billowing smoke over the rooftops. It stung my nostrils and made me cough. An easterly wind was blowing, which was fanning the flames.

'I quickly dressed and rushed down to my parents' bedchamber and woke them, then I woke my two younger brothers, who were asleep in the workshop on the ground floor. They all dressed frantically and Mother quickly took up my baby sister Kate from the cradle next to her bedside. We looked out of the windows at the thickening smoke and knew we had no choice but to pack up and leave. Our house, like most of the others in our street, was built of wood.

'I fetched the handcart from the yard and brought it

73

round to the front door. By now I could feel the heat from the fire burning at my skin. We piled in everything of value; my father's tools, the finished and half-finished gloves from the workshop and the storeroom behind, the few pieces of pewter, Mother's tapestries and our best clothes. I threw in my journal.' He drained the rest of the gourd of water, and wiped his forehead. 'I would never leave my journal.

'We made our way through throngs of people to a large open area called Moorfields, outside the city walls, and made a temporary camp from sticks and drapes. The heat from the fire suffocated me, even out there.

'The next morning Father and I went back to our home. Our street was burned to the ground, a few timbers still burning. We couldn't even get close. It was the worst day of my life. All my family survived the outbreak of plague the previous year, when so many died in London, only to lose their livelihood in the fire.'

Anika took his hand and stroked it gently.

He turned to her. 'Father couldn't afford to support me so I joined a fisherman on the Thames. Do you know what I fished for?'

She shook her head.

'Oysters.'

They both smiled.

'Although there were no pearls in ours. They were sold at Billingsgate fish market. Londoners love eating oysters. I took what money I could to Father and he set up a temporary shop on the ruins of the house. They slept in the local church and I lived on the fishing boat with Samuel. He was slow, but kind enough to me and he taught me to sail.'

Anika looked puzzled, 'So how did you come to be in Port Royal?'

'One morning in October I decided to try my luck in Jamaica. Many were going as indentured servants but I didn't want to enslave myself to some rich merchant, even with the promise of land when the five years were up. I took a cabin boy post. I could fish, I could sew and I loved the sea.

'I sailed on a British navy ship. It was a hard life and I learnt much about sailing a ship. England was at war with the Netherlands and we were attacked by a Dutch merchant ship off Cape Finistere. We had more cannon, fought them off and arrived in Port Royal in June 1667.

'Since then I've worked as a pot boy for Jameson and have been his cabin boy and now I'm with the new tavern keeper, Rutherford. I want no more piracy, but the share I took I'll keep and I'm saving my money. I would like to own some land and grow all manner of fruits.

Father is hoping to rebuild in brick and stone this year, but I doubt he has the money. I promised that one day I would return a rich man and buy them a fine house in London. To this day I have nightmares about fire.'

Anika took his hands in hers and kissed them. 'I'll ask Diego to keep you out of the galley and out on deck.'

As the days wore on and the wind picked up, the ketch clipped through the waves. They sailed on through the night as the wind grew stronger. By four o'clock in the morning Anika lay in her hammock unable to sleep, listening as the wind ripped at the sails and the timbers creaked and moaned. Diego screamed against the wind, 'Strike the sails.'

She hurried up on deck and battled to hammer down the loosened chicken coop, remembering that terrible storm that sank "Black Lady". *Mama you said that May was a good time to sail!* The hens clucked wildly as the waves lifted and dropped the ketch.

The crew scrambled up the rigging and fought with the mainmast sails, then the mizzen. The canvas of the mizzen suddenly tore like a piece of paper and fluttered useless in the gale. They furled the remaining sails as the ship pitched more violently in the waves.

Diego screamed out again. 'Sean, Robbie, tie yourselves onto the masts. Everybody else below and batten down the hatches.'

Where had Diego learnt such skills? Anika did as she was told, as did the others, and scrambled below to make sure the fire was out in the galley, praying her mother might sleep through this night.

Torrential rain fell and lashed the ship so that they could do nothing now but wait for the storm to pass. The ketch tossed like a toy in the seething water. Anika relived "Black Lady's" final moments: the screams of the men as it disappeared under the sea, bow first, as she swam for her life to the Spanish salvage ship.

She knelt and prayed to Saint Elmo, the patron saint of sailors, to save them, as the rain whipped her face and hands. She was not the first, nor would she be the last sailor to pray at sea in such a storm.

CHAPTER 9

By noon the next day the crew sprawled on the weather deck exhausted and silent. The wind was dying down as Anika struggled down the ladder and relit the fire in the galley. Murphy had been swept overboard in the raging seas, the rope that tied him to the mainmast severed.

Once the fire was alight Anika crept into her mother's cabin. 'Are you alright Mama? You look very pale.'

Her mother nodded, sitting up painfully. 'I slept very well.' She looked ghostly.

'I'll bring you some chowder soon Mama.' She would tell her about Murphy when her mother felt stronger.

Later, as Anika hauled in the fishing net to find it torn to shreds, she heard Diego talking to the crew and went over to listen. 'We've been blown way off course. Now we must find land to take on fresh supplies.' He pointed down at the deck, to the large chart held at the corners with cannonballs. 'Worse, we have many ripped sails which will slow us down.'

Stephen spoke out. 'We could try to reach these islands here.' He pointed to a small group of islands off Cuba.

Diego nodded. 'We sail for the Isles de Pinos but now Stephen will show us all how to mend sails and this evening we will have a service for Murphy. I will take his fiddle and his other belongings back to his lady in Port Royal.'

It was a sad group that sat on the deck and patched sails. They had all loved mad, scarecrow Murphy in their separate ways and he had become a good sailor. The sea could be a cruel place. Diego took a mourning ring from his finger and told of the loss of his brother, Pedro, in a storm off North Carolina and Anika remembered her dead brother, Daniel, as she did every day.

As they sailed towards the white palm-fringed beach Anika smelt the roasting pork, blown towards them on the wind. As they drew closer she spotted the buccaneers grilling the slabs of meat over a fire sunk into the fine sand, heard the drunken singing and fear hit her deep in the pit of the stomach. There was no sailing back. They needed fresh supplies, especially water.

Diego gave the order to drop anchor and they all rowed ashore in the pinnace. As the pirates staggered to the water's edge to meet them Anika recognised their language as French. None of the crew spoke French, so by signs it was explained they had come for water, fruit and meat.

The pirates grinned and chattered and shouted and handed out slabs of barbecued pork and passed around tankards of rum. They were the friendliest cut-throats Anika had ever met and the reason soon became clear. Escorted by six brutish-looking men they were taken to see a treasure trove of gold, silver and jewels, guarded by four more pirates; enough to ransom a King. They must have taken a haul from a Spanish galleon and they were celebrating. Some held a mock trial: the pirates faced execution by hanging, but were freed by the drunken, wigged judge perched high in a palm tree. This caused much raucous laughter.

Anika realized that as there were about thirty pirates, all armed with knives and cutlasses, they saw nothing to fear from a few crewmen, a girl, a boy and a sick woman. Nevertheless their Captain did train his telescope on the ketch from time to time and pointing towards the treasure seemed to be asking if they had captured any prizes. Anika knew that pirates were forever greedy. In Port Royal they had no sooner moored their ship, than they were in the taverns drinking and gambling away all they had stolen and were ready for the next chase. She also knew that, fired with strong drink, they could be violent and use torture on their victims.

Diego gathered his crew together and told them he was anxious to be away by nightfall. Everyone set to work. They picked bunches of bananas, hacked down coconuts and filled their barrels with water from the nearby river, then loaded the pinnace. The pirates gave them more slabs of pork.

Anika watched horrified as Robbie turned a turtle on its back and left it there in the baking sun, presumably until they were ready to take it aboard and cook it for its meat. The poor thing had only come ashore to feed. She waited until Robbie had gone and turned the turtle onto his flippers and watched him push away the sand and head slowly to the sea.

The pirates got drunker and began to argue amongst themselves. One weasly man with charred stumps for teeth shouted and pushed a taller man, who unsheathed his cutlass. The weasel pulled out his sword and they fought, stumbling in the soft sands. Another fight broke out, fists this time, and suddenly it was mayhem with all the pirates fighting one another.

Diego beckoned the crew and they stealthily climbed back into the pinnace and rowed with all their strength back to the ketch.

The next days of sailing and mending the sails were below blue skies and a fresh breeze. As Anika knelt on the main deck the sail spread all around her she found it hard to concentrate on stitch after stitch. Diego had told them they were only leagues from the site of the Spanish wreck, the "Don Carlos" and the sunken pirate ship.

As she sewed she ran over in her mind all that she had learnt about sailing a ship. She knew the running of a galley, that was for sure; how many logs to place in the brick oven, how to keep the temperature up. Her Mama had taught her about the use of herbs and spices. Stephen taught her to patch canvas sails and she was slow but fairly proficient. Most of all she wanted to learn how to sail the ship: about navigation, steering and rigging.

In the last week she had watched Diego with his quadrant, his charts and dividers. Her Mama called it African magic, voodoo. *How did he know, in all this expanse of sea, that they were nearly to the wreck site?* She was determined to find out.

Anika folded the mended sail and stored it below in the sail locker. She found Diego in his cabin, relaxing with a jug of ale and asked him the questions that had so troubled her.

He answered her simply. 'All this I use.' He pointed to the compass and astrolabe and backstaff. 'They give me, how you say, our place on the earth on a line from the North Pole to the South Pole. At night I can do this by finding the North Star and making sums from that. In the day I can use the sun.' He picked up the backstaff and laid it to his shoulder. 'If I do this I can take the measurements without looking at the sun.

'My uncle taught me good. I have his maps and charts made by other sailors and I have the waves, the currents, even the birds. They do not like fly too far from land.'

'Will you teach me how to sail Diego? I don't want to spend the rest of my life in the galley.'

He looked out of the stern portholes over the sea,' But of course and you will be good pupil, but now Anika you will not be in the galley because you are most important person on "Pearl". Only you can dive to "Don Carlos".' He took her by the hand, led her up to the weather deck and turned to her with fear in his eyes. 'Do not dive too deep. I do not wish to lose you because you are like daughter to me.'

She smiled and nodded, knowing that he could never replace her Papa, but could be a father to her now. They both looked towards the reef, just visible above the surface with a foam of milky white water playing about it. He laughed and called to the crew out on the deck, 'The Spanish they help us. Look it is the right place because they leave us a marker.'

Anika smiled to see the barrel still tied to the reef.

She prepared to dive in a new spot, but close to the reef. Taking a deep breath, she gripped a cannonball and plunged from the ship down into the blue depths with about a minute to locate the wreck. The stone ball pulled her down. Strutting spider crabs, like a long-legged army protecting their territory, scuttled over the reef, fanned by the delicate branches of the pink coral.

Yes there it was, about eighty feet down. "Don Carlos" lay there with timbers strewn everywhere and an anchor nestled in the sand. She guessed by the location of the anchor that this was the stern, which held the Captain's cabin and the treasure. Letting go of the cannonball, she shot to the surface. It was the deepest she had ever dived and sharp pains stabbed her chest as she swam for "Pearl".

Everyone sat around the deck for the meeting, even Anika's mother had been carried up to take part, which was unusual, as she barely left her cabin due to the sleeping sickness that now claimed her.

Diego spoke clearly. 'Anika has found "Don Carlos" wreck. It is scattered about the reef over there.' He pointed to the swirl of water above the tip of the reef and they tried to imagine what only Anika had seen.

She sang inside because she could help them all. If there was gold down there, just a little would keep them from the slavery her Mama had endured, the slavery that she feared would be the Caribbean's fate.

Diego looked around at all of them. 'What I need to

know is if Anika should keep diving. You can see she pale and weak already. It very dangerous as she will need to stay down even long to bring up gold. We can make a living through trade. We do not need Spanish riches and none of us can help her.'

There was silence.

'All who think Anika should dive at this great depth raise your hands.'

Nobody raised their hand.

Anika smiled around at them, rose to her feet and picked up one of the cannonballs stacked by the rails. Stephen and Diego rushed towards her but she took a deep breath and plunged from the ketch.

She swam straight for the anchor and there behind rocks lay a broken casket, half buried in the white sand. Dropping the ball, she tore open the lid and stuffed emeralds, rubies and pearls into the purse at her waist and pulled the thongs tight.

She grabbed more in her hands and shot to the surface. With all her strength she swam for the ketch, where Diego pulled her aboard. She collapsed on the deck, surrounded by the jewels that would secure her mother's future, all their futures. *Yes it belonged to the Spanish but they had murdered and enslaved her peoples and stolen from them. Let them find it if they could.* Her arms and legs ached with the effort and she felt herself slipping away.

Stephen pummelled her chest to revive her and screamed 'Anika'.

Slowly she opened her eyes and smiled up at him. He helped her to sit up and they all stared at the jewels she had scattered on the decking like a game of marbles and they whooped with joy, embracing and dancing. Diego stopped for breath and called for rum. 'It is time to go home. We will share the treasure later in Port Royal, like good pirates. The Spaniards will be back with their own divers, but they will never find the wreck because nobody can dive like Anika.'

Anika smiled and turned to Stephen. 'This treasure will buy freedom. Perhaps one day the peoples of this earth will seek to make it a place where that is not necessary. It will also buy a new house for your family in London, so they do not live on the charred ruins of their home. A few emeralds will buy peace from Antonio and I am sure he will skulk back to Spain. It has always been his dream.

'Tomorrow I will dive to find "Black Lady" to say my goodbyes. I will search for the bell and Jameson's treasure chest.'

Stephen shook his head wearily. He knew he could not stop her.

CHAPTER 10

Florida Keys, April, 2013

The policeman at the waterfront station in Key West sat at his desk swilling his bottled water. He looked up in amazement at Anna standing in the doorway in her wet suit, dripping water and swaying with fatigue. She clutched her mask and flippers in her hands.

The golden boy policeman stood up to his towering height, hours in the gym showing clearly through his short sleeved white shirt. He looked like a lifeguard and he caught her just before she fell. Throwing a towel around her, he laid her on the sofa he used when on the night shift.

To Anna it felt like heaven to lie down, yet every muscle ached. He covered her with a blanket and she heard him phone for a doctor. He brewed coffee, sliced bread, opened a can and made a tuna sandwich, then made a telephone call. 'Police Sergeant Wayne Wilkins here. Tell Scott this is going to be a busy day, so no time for that work-out and swim but I'll catch him tomorrow. Have a nice day.' Putting the phone down, he slicked back his hair in the mirror.

Anna smelt the coffee and she talked, words spilling over one another, as she struggled off the sofa and out of the wet suit, which she dropped on the floor. It felt good to be comfortable in her shorts and t- shirt.

'Now hang on a minute Miss. Let's start from the beginning and go to the end. So what's the story?'

His eyes widened as she told him that she had been held hostage by sea pirates. Her eyes widened as he told her every officer in Southern Florida was looking for her. She took a long drink of the strong coffee, then explained how the pirates had taken the wreck site documents and laptop and how she had tricked them into letting her dive and swam for the shore.

'I struggled up the beach and a young couple brought me here, but they didn't want to come inside.' She paused to munch the tuna sandwich, which like all American sandwiches seemed to consist of a whole tuna fish and a loaf of white bread. 'You must stop the pirates because they'll ruin the site. They're only interested in the gold.'

His eyes lit up. 'Gold?'

'Yes, and precious jewels.' She found her waterproof purse on the floor, unzipped it and pulled out the sheet of old paper. 'Here's the inventory. The one piece of evidence my Dad doesn't have. He keeps copies of everything, and Tim backs up everything put on the laptops, but this is special. I took it while they weren't looking. This lists what was loaded onto the Spanish galleon in Cartagena, Colombia.'

The policeman took another swig of water. 'So you say there's gold on this old wreck? That'll be the property of the United States Government.'

'Exactly. That's why you have to send patrol boats out there right now to guard the site.'

To her amazement he nodded, telephoned and arranged it, then leant back in his chair. 'First off I thought you might be another illegal immigrant washed up on our beaches from the Caribbean and that I should involve the C & I, but some instinct soon told me you weren't.' He smiled at her, showing perfect white teeth. 'You must call your family.'

He passed her the phone and Anna rang her Dad's mobile. 'Dad?'

'Oh thank God. Where are you?'

'I'm at the Key West Police Station on the waterfront.'

'Are you alright?'

'I'm fine Dad.'

'I'll be over straight away.'

She put down the phone as it clicked. 'Got a can of Coke please?'

He shook his head. 'Don't drink the stuff. No good for you,' and he handed her a bottle of spring water.

'Now tell me about these pirates,' and he turned to his computer screen. 'What did they look like?'

She answered all his questions and settled down on the sofa to read the inventory, only to find it written in archaic Spanish. She barely understood one word.

* * *

A few hours later they were back on "Seeker", over the wreck site. She had made her statement, had interviews with senior policemen and was glad to leave; even more pleased about her new wet suit, which, after examining it, the police had let her keep.

It was lunch-time and Jason had prepared a crisp Caesar salad. Everyone sat around the deck, relaxed and happy and heard her escape story. Anna could not eat a thing and told her father about the giant tuna sandwich.

'It was this big.'

'How big?'

It became an angler's tale. 'But this is what I really want to tell you about.' She pulled the parchment from her purse, waved it in the air and knew that she had everyone's attention. 'It's the inventory of the "Don Carlos".'

Her father turned pale.' Where on earth did you get that?'

'I stole it from them.'

He raised his eyebrows, then leant forward eagerly. 'What does it say?'

'I don't know. I tried to read it but we don't do Spanish at school so I can't make out one word.' She handed it to her father.

He scanned it quickly and then looked up at the expectant faces.

'We have a treasure horde here. No wonder our Spanish friend was interested. The "Don Carlos" sailed from Havana in Cuba for Spain with the rest of the annual treasure fleet on 17 March 1668, trying to avoid the hurricane season. The galleon was loaded in Cartagena, Colombia. It had on board one hundred and fifty gold ingots, nine hundred silver ingots, mostly from the Potesi silver mine in Peru, a casket of uncut emeralds from Colombia, various gold and silver artefacts, jewellery and coins belonging to the passengers, plus a cargo of rosewood and tobacco.'

Jonathan shook his head in amazement. 'I read somewhere that the Spanish sent pearl divers down to salvage the wreck.' He looked up and smiled around. 'Well everyone I think it's time for us to salvage the wreck. We have a great deal to do and now we are protected.' They all looked towards the roar of three oncoming police speedboats and grinned at the divers. 'The US government has clearly been informed of the value of the treasure.'

Anna struggled into her new wet suit and tingled with excitement. Her father was allowing her to go down with the divers as long as she stayed close to them and kept in radio contact. Alysia strapped air cylinders to Anna's back and then Anna pulled on her flippers.

Jodie looked at Anna with admiration. 'You really look the part. I'd be terrified I'd run out of air or something. I'll catch you later,' and she prepared to lounge on the deck and listen to 'One Direction' on her iPod. Anna knew Jodie had never really been interested enough to want to learn to Scuba dive, but everyone was different.

Anna checked her radio and pulled on her mask, then gave Jodie the thumbs up. She plunged over the side with Jason, Pete and Alysia and swam down into the crystal clear water. This time there were no pirates, only three globular pink jellyfish. She swam over the site, mapped out in a grid system and Jason, the illustrator, began his work recording the timbers within each square of the grid. Pete criss-crossed with a metal detector and signalled to Alysia that he had located something and she searched the soft white sand with the airlift. As the sand filtered away he discovered a tankard and a plate. Anna found a spoon and she remembered the model of the galleon with the crew eating their meal.

When Jason had recorded the finds they were lifted and Anna placed the spoon carefully in her bag. She swam on and then she spotted a human bone. She signalled to Jason and murmured a prayer as he drew it. This was a grave site and many men had lost their lives here.

Should she be there at all? It was the first time she had asked herself that question and would need time to reflect and find her answer. Tim had spoken of 'virtual retrieval', where the site is left relatively undisturbed and electronic imaging giving a 3-D image of the wreck is the main priority.

She spoke into her radio to the control room. ' "Seeker", this is Anna. I've found a human bone. I'll bring it up for analysis.'

'Well done You've got another fifteen minutes then you must come up.'

She swam on nearer the reef, shoals of striped angel fish swimming with her. It was wonderful, until she spotted the shoal of barracuda. Some of them were almost two metres long, jaws with daggers for teeth and they were swimming straight towards her. She stared back in horror when suddenly they changed direction and, in a shimmer of silver, swam off to the right. Her heart thumped in her chest and she steadied herself against the coral. Slowly she began to search again.

She dug in the sand with her hands and touched metal. Another cannon. No it was more bell-shaped.

Bell shaped! Her heart leapt again and she scrabbled in the sand, like a crab hiding from predators. It was the ship's bell! She radioed in the news to screams of joy and congratulations from the control room.

CHAPTER 11

The following morning Anna watched as the cast iron bell hung precariously over the deck, hoisted on strong ropes by the salvage crane. She held her breath, as did the entire team, as the crane lowered the ship's bell gently to the deck. Jonathan slid the ropes off and patted the bell like a long-lost friend. It was heavily encrusted with barnacles, but as luck would have it the first attempts at removing the debris with a chisel revealed an engraving.

Anna wished her father was here to see this but he had gone to Key Largo to visit the library and the Maritime Museum. He thought there might just be some information there and they had no time to lose. He told her time was money, which sounded very American but she knew that he was right. The whole operation was costing a fortune; hire of divers, the salvage ship with all the latest electronic equipment.

Jonathan turned to Anna. 'Come and read the name and date. You were the one that found her.' Anna rushed forward and concentrating on the beautiful script , read aloud '"Don Carlos", Cadiz 1665'; a cheer went up from the team. She sat down, staring at the bell in amazement. *So the ship had been built in Cadiz, Spain in 1665 and had sunk in May 1668, whilst loaded with treasure from South America.* She felt like a detective.

But what of the people who had sailed in the galleon?

Remembering the spoon in her bag she hurried down to their laboratory, next to the control room to enter the details in the database. Jonathan had made it clear that every find must be logged, with its exact position on the wreck site, ensuring the site was seen as a whole.

She fished out the spoon and washed off the clinging sand. It looked like it was made of silver. *Who could have used it? It must have belonged to somebody wealthy, perhaps the Spanish Captain or a rich passenger.* Turning it over she noticed the maker's mark on the back of the handle, then punched the air with delight. Jonathan and her father would both be able to give an approximate date, but after careful cleaning and analysis in the lab a silver expert could pin it down to the individual maker.

She sat down at the computer. The screen showed the grid system mapping the site into squares. As she entered the code for utensil in the correct square, Tim appeared at her shoulder. 'Thanks Anna. It's starting to make some sense now. Over the next few days when all the timbers have been mapped we may be able to understand the ship's last moments; the way it broke up, what caused it. We think it foundered on the reef in a storm.'

Anna nodded, then added the spoon to the database of finds, got up from the computer and crossed the cabin to a long workbench attached to the wall. She laid it in the tray with the other spoons and knives awaiting conservation.

The next tray held mostly buckles, probably from breeches' straps. Some looked like lumps of rock, but by their shape were thought to be buckles. Only an X-ray would reveal the object. There was also a pair of spectacles, the glass long since broken and lost. The leg bone she had found lay in the tray of human remains. Her Dad had told her it was part of the lower leg, the tibia.

Jodie came skipping down the steps in a turquoise bikini and Anna pointed to the bone. 'I found that yesterday.'

'You mean you touched a dead body? Gruesome.'

'I had to Jodie. We need to know what happened. When it's analysed by paleontologists they can tell the sex, any diseases, injuries. With a complete skeleton they can build up a very good profile of the person.' She realized she was beginning to sound like her Dad.

'Imagine working on old bones every day. I think I'm going to be sick.'

Anna laughed. She could do nothing else. Jodie was her best friend and she had a good point.

As all work in the afternoon concerned raising the cannon Anna found herself with free time. After all the excitement she found that it was just what she needed. She and Jodie swam in the warm Caribbean near the ship and then sunbathed on towels on the deck.

Anna was no expert on female beauty, but as Jodie lay there, her ear plugs in, listening to her iPod, her foot tapping as the music thumped through her head, she thought Jodie was right to want to try to be a model. Why not? It sounded a very glamorous life. Somehow Anna knew that she would lead the opposite life, up to her knees in mud or under the water in silt, because she wanted to leave school and train as a marine archaeologist.

Her father wandered towards them with mango drinks on a tray, ice chinking in the glasses, and set it on the low plastic table. He was grinning like a schoolboy who has just scored the winning goal in an important football match. Jodie took a drink and thanked him, her life complete.

He took off his rucksack and unzipped it. 'Look what I've found!' He pulled out an old book, the leather cover stained and faded, the pages brown. 'The lady archivist has lent it to me, most unprofessional.'

'So you've not lost your charm then Dad,' Anna winked at him.

He pulled on his white gloves, smiling, like a surgeon about to perform an operation and laying it on the table carefully opened it. Anna and Jodie knelt to look.

Written in English in black ink the title page read, "Journal 1665 – 1670" of Stephen Cartwright. Born in London 1654".

Anna had never seen her father so excited. He turned to an entry for 17 March 1668 in a scratchy handwriting and read aloud to them.

"The Captain spied a Spanish galleon today. We sailed in pursuit as the Captain said we could expect a big share each of the prize on this one. He was sure it was one of the treasure fleet separated from the others in the bad weather. We chased her towards the coast of East Florida, but a storm blew out of nowhere and the galleon sank. It was a fearsome sight as there could have been few survivors. We escaped sorely thrashed."

The girls looked at each other in astonishment. Could it be the "Don Carlos"? The date was right and so was the location. Jodie's eyes shone. Anna realised that Jodie had begun to imagine Stephen as she was doing herself. He would have been fourteen. The story he told was becoming real for her.

Her father could hardly contain himself. 'I've only read some of it because I was so keen to get back. You must read it for yourselves, but I have to give it to Jonathan first you understand?'

Both girls nodded.

'But listen to this girls.'

"13 April 1668

Gibbons, the First Officer, said the shipwreck was the "Don Carlos", a Spanish treasure galleon."

The girls clapped their hands in delight as Anna's Dad read on. "Gibbons can't talk about anything more. He was stabbed to death today and the crew believe it was the Captain who murdered him. Murphy says he saw Captain Jameson stab Gibbons. He was above them, up on the rigging. Nobody talks of it. The Captain is a fearsome man.

14 April 1668

Captain Jameson forced Anika to dive and find the wreck of the Spanish galleon. I suspect she found it but she did not admit to it. She is a fine diver for pearls. Two Spanish divers went with her and found a gold necklace.

"16 April 1668

A terrible storm is blowing up. I have no time to write, but must go down to the galley and see how Anika fares. The waves are over the ship's rails."

"19 April 1668

" I thank God that Anika and I are safe and sailing to

Saint Augustine in East Florida in the Spanish salvage ship. Most of the pirates from "Black Lady" are drowned leaving only six, including Murphy and the two Scottish brothers and they are sailing the ship. The Spanish are chained below, complaining loudly at the loss of their ship. Diego, our cook, is safe as is Anika's drunken, so-called stepfather, Antonio. Anika makes plans for us to find the two wrecks one day. I also thank God for preserving my journal from the sea."

Anna sipped her mango juice and felt like a little girl again listening to her favourite bed-time story. Her Dad turned to another page.

"22 September 1668

I thought I was going to lose Anika today. She dived to the "Don Carlos" wreck…'

Her father paused for effect.

Anna could not bear it.

Nor could Jodie. 'Go on James.'

"She brought back emeralds and rubies and pearls, but her poor body could hardly breathe when she came up. Praise be to God she survived it and we are all rich beyond our wildest dreams. She wants to dive on the wreck of our pirate ship "The Black Lady" to find the treasures in the Captain's cabin. I know it will be impossible to stop her, but I do not want her to dive again. I could not bear it if she died."

Anna's Dad looked up from the book and stared out at the turquoise sea. 'So there's another wreck close by: the maggy clearly picked up something. So what happened?' He shook his head and continued reading.

"We will share all the treasure out fairly when we return home to Port Royal."

He put the journal down on his lap and stared into space. 'Port Royal is only a sleepy fishing village now. It's close to Kingston, the capital of Jamaica, so I visited it as a child. My ancestors were sold at the slave market in Kingston.' Anna took hold of his hand as his eyes watered with suppressed tears.

'In the second half of the seventeenth century, when Stephen and Anika lived, Kingston did not exist, but Port Royal grew and became the busiest port in the Caribbean; a haven for pirates. On 7 June 1692, just before midday, an earthquake struck, quickly followed by tidal waves. We know the exact time of the quake because a pocket watch was excavated, the hands frozen at eleven forty three a.m.'

Anna shook her head in disbelief. 'That's amazing. What a find.'

'Two thirds of the town's inhabitants lost their lives in the earthquake and in the weeks to follow died from their injuries and disease. The town never really recovered, so that in the eighteenth century people gradually moved away.'

'Dad, do you think Stephen and Anika were there when the earthquake struck? Let me see,' and she did some mental maths. 'If Stephen was born in 1654 he would have been thirty eight years old when the earthquake struck.'

'I'll see what I can find out.' He turned the stiffened pages, looking for dates, talking as he searched.

'Today Port Royal is what archaeologists call a "catastrophic site" because of that 1692 earthquake. He looked up from the journal. 'What's unusual is that a good deal of the town's remains lie underwater because the tidal waves that followed the earthquake submerged so much. The archeology is only about twenty five feet down below the water: walls and floors, even ships. Developers are making the harbour suitable for cruise ships to dock and the site an underwater tourist attraction, but things move slow in Jamaica, yeh mon, irie.

'Yeh mon?' Anna looked puzzled.

'A Jamaican saying, equivalent to Yes Man. No problem. They have their own patois, their own dialect. There's also a museum in Port Royal; I'll take you both there.'

They were disturbed by clapping and cheering from the weather deck. The cannon was raised and Anna caught the word 'emeralds' in amongst the shouting. The "Don Carlos" was beginning to give up its secrets, but what of " Black Lady"?

'We'll have to leave the journal girls. Come on.'

CHAPTER 12

Night fell and Anna lay in her bunk bed poring over the journal by torchlight. The book was a treasure trove and she felt honoured that Jonathan had lent it to her. The sound of Jodie's regular breathing came from above as she slept peacefully. Anna wore white gloves and as she turned the dusty page she sneezed. Jodie turned over but did not wake. She read one entry over again.

"23 September 1668

"I am in love with Anika and want to marry her. I have reason to hope that she loves me too. She is brave and yet I fear for her when she dives so deep. Today she dived on the wreck of "Black Lady" and found the gold bell and she brought us more jewels from Jameson's casket. She found his silver plate with the initials RJ inscribed and said her goodbyes. She says they were pirates, for one reason or another, but they were still our shipmates. We are all now very wealthy, but it was the day I met Anika that I became a rich man.'

If only history lessons could be like this instead of Mr Watson droning on about treaties and national boundaries. She yawned and looked at her alarm clock. Three a.m. Turning off the lamp she snuggled down to sleep, the journal buzzing in her head.

She turned over restlessly and heard shouts from above. She sat bolt upright, shot out of bed and quickly pulled on her shorts and t-shirt. Jodie slept on; her iPod still plugged into her ears. She crept barefoot up the creaking steps onto the weather deck and stopped dead, stifling the scream that rose in her throat.

Two masked men with revolvers held her father and Jonathan against the rail. None of them had seen her. Ducking back, petrified, she looked across the water at the police patrol boat lit up in the darkness. *Why on earth had the police patrol not responded?*

One of the men held a revolver to Jonathan's temple. The men forced her father and Jonathan at gunpoint down the steps. Anna drew back into the shadows and tiptoed back to her cabin for her iPhone. She pulled it from her bag, hands trembling, dialed 911 and asked for the police.

She whispered into the phone, giving their location and as much information as she could. 'There's a police patrol boat here but they don't seem to be aware. If you could contact them…'

Footsteps started down the steps. She switched off the phone and quickly hid it and the journal under her pillow. Jodie slept peacefully.

Rodrigo stepped into the cabin. 'We meet again Anna, except this time you won't get away.' He pointed the gun at her and for half a terrifying second she thought he was going to shoot her. Rodrigo grabbed Anna by the right arm and dragged her up the steps to the weather deck and down again into the laboratory.

All the ship's crew and team were there, shaken from sleep and herded against the wall, two machine guns pointing at them, one held by Doughnut. She took a deep breath and tried not to panic. She was the only one on "Seeker" who knew the police were on their way.

In an instant her world fell apart.

Rodrigo turned to the Captain. 'You, go start the engines. We need to get away from here now.'

Charlie stared him out and did not budge.

One of the thugs stepped forward and shoved a machine gun into his back, 'Move.' Charlie slowly climbed the steps.

Rodrigo smiled a thin smile. 'We've taken care of the police patrol boat up there; posed as tourists who had run out of fuel.' He looked at Anna and laughed. 'An old trick of ours. We drugged them and tied them up, but we don't want to be here when they wake up now do we?'

Jonathan blurted out, 'But there were three patrol boats.'

'Not when we arrived. The others must have been called away; perhaps to an urgent meeting at one of the bars in Key West.'

He beckoned to one of the thugs. 'Tell Pedro to follow us in the speedboat and keep his eyes open. We'll stay on this old tub and pack up what they've collected so far.'

He laughed again and picked up the gold coins in the tray. 'We'll be back for the rest of course when all the heat dies down. We have the exact site of the wreck.' He turned to Anna. 'We thank you for all that little girl.'

Anna glared at him.

He pointed to the bell of the "Don Carlos". 'That should fetch a bit in South America where not so many questions are asked. One of the Colombian drug barons will be very happy to have that in his villa as a doorbell.'

Anna heard the engines throb and the ship began to

cut the water. She looked across at her father who was haggard and she rushed over to him. He hugged her and kept holding her close.

'Another thing little girl. You have something of mine.'

Anna knew he meant the inventory; Jonathan had copied it and Tim had entered it in the database. She had no choice but to hand it over to Rodrigo. *Where were the police? They were going to be too late.* The ship chugged steadily now and she had no idea where they were headed.

Tim asked if he could use the computer. Rodrigo laughed and lit a cigar. ' Are you crazy? When we drop you off on a pretty Paradise Island you'll have plenty chance to use it then.'

The ship made good progress and Anna knew there was no hope of the police finding them in the night. Rodrigo had all the blinds pulled and the lights on deck were out. Everyone was being watched. If anyone had a mobile phone in here they had no chance to use it.

Rodrigo ran his fingers through the pieces of eight in one of the trays whilst his thugs trained their guns on everybody. Then he spotted the other tray. The four uncut emeralds glinted up at him turning his face green, the wooden casket that held them long since rotted to practically nothing.

Anna turned to the doorway and shouted, 'WOW Jodie I love your new PJs.' All the thugs and Rodrigo turned to look and Jodie screamed. Anna nodded to Tim and he crept, unseen, to the computer to enable the satellite navigation system, knowing the "Seeker" would soon be missed. Jodie saw Tim at the computer and went into staged hysterics. Anna held her breath. *The police could track "Seeker", but would it work? Could they catch them?* Anna squeezed Tim's shoulder gently telling him she knew, then crossed to Rodrigo. He was clever and must not see Tim.

'How much is all this treasure worth?'

He puffed at his cigar. 'Pieces of eight probably $300 each on the current market.' He ran his hand through the emeralds. These are worth thousands of dollars each.' He warmed to the subject. 'The whole treasure will be worth *millions*.'

Anna could not resist it. 'You don't care then that you will trample the site and the archaeology will be lost.'

'Oh little girl.' He laughed. 'You just don't get it. He stubbed out the cigar. 'The emerald market… '

Heavy footsteps pounded on the decking above and in seconds six US police burst through the door. 'Drop your weapons.'

The thugs looked up in horror and did as they were told.

Rodrigo forced Anna in front of him and put his revolver to her head. 'I'm taking the girl with me, so put down your guns or she dies.'

Anna dug him in the ribs with her sharp elbows, winded him and ran to her father. The nearest officer swiftly disarmed Rodrigo and the police seemed to be everywhere. 'Put your hands above your heads.' With lightning speed the police handcuffed them all and marched them up the steps to the waiting speedboats, Rodrigo protesting loudly that he needed his lawyer.

Anna's Dad called after him. 'You'll need a lawyer

alright Rodrigo, because the United States government is going to throw the book at you.' He turned to Anna and hugged her tightly. 'Well done love. You're a star. How about fixing us hot chocolates?

'Sounds like a plan Dad.'

* * *

As dawn broke another day's diving lay ahead of them. Everyone was excited and worked as a team. Anna found her father and read him Stephen's last journal entry:

"31 December 1670

This is my last journal entry, as I find myself too busy with the land to write much these days, so I will attempt to sum up my year. The weather here in East Florida is good for the banana crop so we prosper well and trade our crop for goods from England. I am trying to grow pineapples, a much-loved fruit there.

Anika and I are to marry in the new year. Anika's Mama continues to improve, although she is still a little frail. She received a letter in June from Antonio's brother saying that Antonio had died a few weeks before of smallpox.

Anika dives here sometimes because she loves to visit the coral reefs. She has made a necklace of her pearls and gave me a pearl teardrop ear-ring as a Christmas gift. We never returned to the 'Don Carlos" wreck, but no doubt one day someone will find her and " Black Lady." Good fortune to them. We have no wish to return again to Port Royal."

'They would have left Port Royal years before the earthquake Anna.'

She nodded happily. 'It's a wonderful journal Dad. It's made me think how glad I am that I keep a diary. Perhaps somebody will read about our expedition in years to come.'

'You keep up the good work.'

'Where did you find Stephen's diary?'

'The archivist remembered a journal she had read. She took me down lanes of old books and documents and found it for me. If we all work together like that we shall certainly uncover some of the past's secrets. She lent it to me because of the research we are doing, but it must go back today. I said I would take her out for dinner this evening. Do you mind?'

'Of course I don't mind,' and she squeezed his arm. She had always hoped he might meet someone. She knew how much he missed her Mum.

Anna handed the journal to her father. 'I'd best get back to work then Dad as Jodie's already marking finds. Life is full of surprises!' They walked into the busy laboratory to see Jodie with a black marker pen in one hand and a collar bone in the other. Anna winked at her Dad and hurried over to the trays.

* * *

The next day Anna pulled on her wet suit once more. This time the team were looking for "Black Lady", the location now fixed about a quarter of a mile from the "Don Carlos". Fastening on her flippers, she thanked God that Anika and Stephen would not be down there. She heard Stephen's voice in her head and could see Anika's face, her wide-set eyes. Stephen had described it all and she could not bear to find remains of their bodies.

She was searching for people's lives, not artefacts, but only archaeology and historical documents could piece it back together. It was all like a mammoth three-dimensional jigsaw puzzle.

Jodie appeared beside her. 'I wish I was coming with you.'

Anna gave her a hug. 'We'll ask Dad if you can start to work for your diving certificate tomorrow. It only takes a few days and we're here for a while yet.'

Jodie nodded while Anna put on her mask and checked her radio. She plunged into the water alongside Alysia, Pete and Jason. They swam down to about thirty metres and Anna marvelled at Anika. *How could she have done it? Her courage was out of this world and her stamina truly awe-inspiring.*

They soon spotted the wreck of an old ship, and swam over it. Anna had a strong sense of Anika's presence. She dived here for Captain Jameson's treasure. Anna knew they had found "Black Lady", but the divers needed more than that. Pete crackled on the radio back to the control room. '"Seeker", this is Pete. It looks seventeenth century by the shape of the hull, probably a three-masted English vessel.'

Jonathan came over the radio. 'Roger that Pete. That fits with the journal. Stephen says Jameson took the ship from the English in September 1667 and renamed her " Black Lady". All look for the bell. We know how good Anna is at that.'

It was as though someone took Anna's hand and guided her over the wreck. She knew she would find the bell because she was being taken there. As the crabs scuttled away and the stingrays swam around her, brushing her legs with their velvety skin, Anna came to the spot and stopped. She shifted the sand with her hands. *Dig deeper.* Her fingers touched a metal object and scrabbling wildly to remove the centuries of sand, she uncovered the bell. It was made of solid gold and lay unblemished. She read " Black Lady 1668".

Scattered around it lay rubies and emeralds in their thousands, pieces of eight, silver ingots, Jameson's personal treasure, property of the US government. Anna smiled as she radioed the control room.

The site was her treasure trove and she continued searching.